DAVE FEARLESS AND THE CAVE OF MYSTERY

BY

ROY ROCKWOOD

DAVE FEARLESS AND THE CAVE OF MYSTERY

CHAPTER I

SPLENDID FORTUNE

"It's gone! It's gone!"

"What is gone, Dave?"

"The treasure, Bob."

"But it was on board--in the boxes."

"No--those boxes are filled with old iron and lead. We have been tricked, robbed! After all our trouble, hardship, and peril, I fear that the golden reward we counted on so grandly has slipped from our grasp."

It was on the deck of the Swallow, moored in the harbor of a far-away Pacific Ocean tropical island, that Dave Fearless spoke. He had just rushed up from the cabin in a great state of excitement.

Below loud, anxious, and angry voices sounded. As one after another of the officers and sailors appeared on the deck, all of them looked pale and perturbed.

What might be called a terrific, an overwhelming discovery had just been made by Captain Paul Broadbeam and by Dave's father, Amos Fearless, the veteran ocean diver.

For two weeks, after a hard battle with the sea and its monsters, after fighting savages and piratical enemies, the beautiful steamer, the Swallow, had plowed through sun-tipped waves, favored by gentle breezes, homeward-bound.

Every heart on board had been light and happy. Labeled and sealed on the sandy floor of the ballast room, lay four boxes believed to contain over half a million dollars in gold coin.

Legally this vast treasure belonged to Amos and Dave Fearless, father and son. To those who had aided and protected them, however, from Doctor Barrell, on board the Swallow to make deep-sea soundings and secure specimens of rare marine monsters for the United States Government, down to Bob Vilett, Dave's chosen chum and the ambitious young assistant engineer of the vessel, every soul on board knew that when they reached San Francisco, the generous ocean diver and his son would make a most liberal division of the splendid fortune they had fished up in mid-ocean.

As said, the serenity of these fond hopes was now rudely blasted. Dave, rushing up on deck quite pale and agitated, had made the announcement that brought Bob to his feet with a shock.

They were two sturdy boys. The flavor of the briny deep was manifest in their bronzed faces, their attire, their clear bright eyes, and sinewy muscles. They had known hardship and peril such as make men resolute and brave. Although Dave was deeply distressed, determination rather than despair was indicated in the way in which he took the bad, bad news now being conveyed with lightning speed, mostly with depressing effect, all through the ship.

Bob Vilett steadied himself against a capstan and stared in silence at his chum. Dave's hand grasped the bow rail with an iron grip, as if thereby seeking to relieve his tense feelings. His eyes were directed away from Bob, away from the ship, fixedly, almost sternly, scanning the ocean stretch that spread almost inimitably towards the west. It seemed as if mentally he was going back over the long course they had just pursued, never dreaming that they were carrying a ballast of worthless old junk instead of the royal fortune on which they had fondly counted.

"Well, all I've got to say," observed Bob at length, with a great sigh, "is that it's pretty tough."

"I fancy," responded Dave, in a set, thoughtful way, "it's a case of three times and out. We fished it up--one. We've lost it--two. We must find it again--three. That's all."

"You're dreaming!" vociferated Bob. "Say, Dave Fearless, you're a genius and a worker, but if you mean that there is the least hope in the world in going back over a course of over a thousand miles hunting up men with a two weeks' start of us--desperate men, too--scouring a trackless ocean for fellows who have to hide, and know how to do it, why, it's--bosh!"

"Bob Vilett," said Dave, with set lip and unflinching eye, "we are only boys, but we have tried to act like men, and Captain Broadbeam respects us for it. We have his confidence. He is old, not much of a thinker, but brave as a lion and ready for any honest, logical suggestion. Here's a dilemma, a big one. You and I--young, quick, ardent--we must think for him. We have been robbed. We must catch the thieves. We must recover that treasure. Where's the best and surest, and the quickest way to do it? Put on your thinking-cap, Bob, and try and do some of the hardest brain work of your life."

"Hold on--where are you going?" demanded Bob, as his chum went away over into a remote corner of the bow and sat down on an isolated water barrel.

But Dave only waved his hand peremptorily, almost irritably, at Bob. His chum knew that it would be useless to renew the conversation just now. He had seen Dave in just such a mood on other occasions--it was when affairs were going wrong and needed straightening out.

"All right," murmured Bob resignedly, moving over to where some glum-faced sailors were discussing the disappointment of the hour in a group. "It won't hurt any of us to have Dave Fearless do some of that tall thinking of his. Oh, dear! All that money gone. And after all we went through to get it!"

Meanwhile Dave Fearless sat posed like a statue. His gaze was fixed beyond the little inlet where the Swallow was moored, straight across the unbroken ocean stretch. His thoughts just then, however, were not fixed on the west, but rather on the east. A vivid panorama of his stirring adventures of the past few months seemed spread out to his mental eye. They went back to the start of what the present moment seemed to be the finish.

Dave's home was at Quanatack, along the coast of Long Island Sound. There for many years his father had been an expert master diver, and Dave himself, reared beside the sea and loving it, had done service as a lighthouse assistant.

In the first volume of the present series, entitled "The Rival Ocean Divers," it was told how they one day learned that they were direct heirs of the Washington family, who twenty years previous had acquired a fortune of nearly a million dollars in China. This, all in gold coin, had been shipped in the Happy Hour for San Francisco. A storm overtook the vessel, which sunk in two miles of water in mid-ocean with the treasure aboard.

Amos Fearless secured a chart showing the exact location of the wreck. Unfortunately two distant relatives, a miserly trickster named Lem Hankers and his worthless son, Bart, learned of the sunken treasure, too. They proceeded to San Francisco and were joined by a rascally partner named Pete Rackley. The trio chartered from a wrecking company the Raven, Captain Nesik in command, and engaged a professional diver named Cal Vixen.

The Fearlesses, learning of this, hastened their plans. An old friend of the diver, Captain Broadbeam, was just then starting out with the Swallow, to convey a well-known scientist from Washington to mid-ocean. The Swallow was equipped with the finest diving bells and apparatus for capturing and preserving rare monsters of the deep. Broadbeam agreed to incidentally assist Amos Fearless in the search for the sunken treasure.

The rival divers located this at about the same time. Thrilling experiences followed, terrific battles with submarine monsters, hair-breadth perils on the ocean bed. The Hankers and their diver after several efforts gave up the quest. Dave and his father stuck at it until one day they located the hull of the Happy Hour. Bag after bag of gold they stored in their Costell diving bell, until all the treasure was conveyed safely to the hold of the Swallow. Then they set sail for home.

Pete Rackley had managed to secrete himself aboard. He disabled the machinery of the Swallow. This was the starting-point of a new series of adventures as related in our second volume, "The Cruise of the Treasure Ship."

It now became plot and warfare on the part of the disgruntled Hankers and their friends. The result was that one dark and foggy night the schemers succeeded in stealing aboard of the Swallow. Captain Broadbeam, Bob Vilett, Doctor Barrell, and the Fearlesses were put ashore on a lonely island, and the Raven steamed away with the captured convoy.

A sixth person was also marooned. This was one Pat Stoodles, a whimsical Irishman, who had been previously rescued by the Swallow from this same island, where for several years he had been the king of its savage inhabitants.

"The Cruise of the Treasure Ship" has told graphically of the many adventures of the marooned. Stoodles reassumed his kingship temporarily and helped his friends out of many a sore dilemma. A cyclone and an earthquake drove all hands to a neighboring island. Finally Dave and Bob discovered the Swallow, somewhat dismantled, lying off the coast of the island. They boarded her to find Mr. Drake, the boatswain, Mike Conners, the cook, and Ben Adams, the engineer, handcuffed in the cabin. These men had refused to navigate the Swallow for Captain Nesik. They told how the cyclone had parted the two vessels and the Swallow had been driven to her present isolated moorings. They told also of the four boxes into which they had seen the Hankers place the sunken treasure.

For a second time, believing their enemies and the Raven lost in the storm, the Fearless party started homeward. Incidentally they had enabled a worthy young fellow named Henry Dale to earn a large sum by towing with them a lost derelict ship. This they had turned over to an ocean liner they met. Then, the Swallow needing some repairs, they had headed for Minotaur Island, their present port of moorage.

This island had originally belonged to the government of Chili. Just now, however, it was claimed by Peru, and was also in a certain state of rebellion. The governor was a miserly and tricky individual, and had demanded a large sum from Captain Broadbeam before he would let him moor the Swallow.

He sent out as pilot a wretched, drunken fellow, who ran the Swallow into an obscure creek where she struck some obstacle, tearing a hole in her hull.

Thus disabled, Captain Broadbeam found it necessary to shift the various articles in the hold. The four sealed boxes were removed, and Amos Fearless naturally suggested that they take a look at their golden fortune.

Ten minutes later the startling discovery was made which has been recorded in the opening lines of the present chapter--

The great Washington fortune was not, as had all along been supposed, aboard of the Swallow.

CHAPTER II

FOUL PLAY

Captain Paul Broadbeam came up on deck, his face red as a peony, his brow dark as a thundercloud.

He was manifestly irritated. In his great foghorn bass voice he gave out a dozen quick orders. His evident intention was to break up the little groups discussing the happening of the hour.

"Avast there!" he roared to a special set of four seamen they had taken on at Mercury Island a week previous. "No mutinous confabs allowed here. If you expected something never promised, that's your lookout. Those that can't be satisfied with plain square wages can take their kits ashore."

Amos Fearless had followed the captain from the cabin. The veteran ocean diver looked greatly disappointed and distressed. He made out Dave and went over to where he sat.

"Well, my son," he said, disturbing Dave's deep reverie by placing a trembling hand on his shoulder, "this is a bad piece of news."

"Yes, father," replied Dave gravely.

"We've been big fools," continued Amos Fearless, with a sigh and a dejected shake of his head. "Might better have kept to our sure pay back at Quanatack. We are only humble folk, Dave, and should have been satisfied with our lot. Might have known million-dollar fortunes don't come falling on such as we, except in story-books."

"Wrong, father!" said Dave sharply. "I don't look at it that way at all. We are the legal Washington heirs, and had a right to expect what was our due. It was a clear-cut, honest piece of business."

"Well, it's turned out worse than nothing for us."

"I don't see that, either," observed Dave. "We went at the matter right. We located the sunken treasure. Someone has stolen it. Surely, father, you don't mean to tell me that you will fold your hands meekly and make no effort to recover the fortune we have worked so hard for? Why, father," declared Dave, with spirit, "all we may have to go through can't begin to be as difficult and dangerous as what we have already accomplished. It looks simple and plain to me--our duty."

"Does it now?" murmured the old diver in a thoughtful way.

"Yes. Someone stole that treasure, and of course it was the Hankers and Captain Nesik and that crew of rascals. Well, father, they can't spend it on a desert island in mid-ocean, can they?"

"Why, I suppose not," said the diver.

"Certainly not. They will try to get back to civilization. Now I have been thinking out the whole matter. Mr. Drake, our boatswain, saw the Hankers make a great show of putting the gold into the four wooden boxes. Now we find out that this was just a pretense to deceive the crew of the Raven. Later, of course, they secretly removed it. To where, father? To the Raven? If so, they ran into a bad predicament. From what the Island Windjammers told Pat Stoodles the last they saw of the Raven she was scudding along in the cyclone, completely disabled. If she stranded, of course they hurried out the treasure before she sank. Then it is hidden somewhere among those islands where we had our hard fight for existence. The survivors are either waiting there hoping some ship will stray their way, or they fixed up the Raven and are making for the South American coast."

"That's a pretty long talk, but a sensible one, Dave," said the old diver, brightening up a good deal. "Go ahead, my son--supposing all this?"

"Yes, father," said Dave, "supposing all this."

"Well, what then?"

"Why, the next thing is to prove I am right or partly right. We must go back to the Windjammers' Island and hunt for a trace of the Raven. Stoodles can make his old subjects, the natives, tell what they know. If we find that the Raven was not wrecked and has made for the South American coast, then we must put right after them."

"Dave, you give me a good deal of courage," said Amos Fearless--"you make me ashamed of my despair. I'm old, though, you see, and this is a big disappointment."

"Don't you fret, father. I feel certain that prompt work will soon put us on the track of the treasure."

"I'll speak to Captain Broadbeam right away," said the old diver, and Dave was pleased to see how nimbly his father started off, encouraged and hopeful from the little talk he had given him.

Bob Vilett had been watching Dave all this time. The young diver did not sit meditating any longer. He had thought out what had to be done. Now he must decide how to do it. He paced up and down with smart steps. Bob started to rejoin him. There was an interruption.

A man half-dressed, one boot on and carrying the other in his hand, came banging up the cabin steps.

"Bad cess to it! Begorra! Who tuk it--who tuk it?" he shouted.

This was Pat Stoodles. He seemed to have just awakened and to have learned of the astounding discovery of the hour. Making out Dave, who was a great favorite with him, Stoodles sprinted with his long limbs across the deck.

"Wirra, now, me broth of a boy, tell me it's false!" implored Pat.

"If you mean that we've got four boxes of junk aboard instead of gold," said Dave, "unfortunately it's true."

"Acushla! luk at that now," groaned Stoodles, throwing up his hands in sheer dismay. "And I was to have had a thousand dollars."

"More than that, Mr. Stoodles," answered Dave. "You have been one of our good loyal friends, and my father has often planned starting you in a nice paying business, had we reached San Francisco with the treasure."

"Hear that, now!" cried Stoodles. "Didn't I write that same thing to my brother in New York? Didn't I tell him I'd be home, loaded down with gold? I sent the letter from Mercury Island. And now I must write him again, telling him it was all a poor foolish old fellow's dream. All I've got is my losht dignity as king of the Windjammers."

Poor Stoodles tore his sparse hair and looked the picture of gloom and discontent.

"I'll write to my brother at once," he resumed. "Have you a postage stamp to spare, Dave?"

"They use the Chilian stamps here, I believe," replied Dave. "You will have to go to the town to get one, Mr. Stoodles."

"I can accommodate you," spoke a brisk, pleasant voice promptly.

All hands turned sharply to view the speaker. Dave, in some surprise, saw a bronzed bright-faced young man coming up a rope ladder swung over the side of the Swallow.

Dave had never seen him before. The newcomer had rowed up the creek in a skiff. Looking down into this, Dave saw an artist's sketching outfit, also a camera.

"Excuse me," said this newcomer, "if I am intruding here. I am a traveling artist out for health and views. Thought I'd take a picture of your ship, if you don't object."

"Not in the least," answered Dave courteously, although the request came at a time when his thoughts were absorbed with more important matters.

"And again," said the young fellow, "I wanted to see some home faces and hear home voices. My name is Adair. I live in Vermont. By the way, though," he continued to Stoodles, taking out a wallet, "you asked for a postage stamp, I believe?"

The speaker ran over the compartments in the wallet. A stray gust of wind caught a little paper fragment it held, blew it up into the air, and Stoodles caught it just as it was being carried over the rail into the water.

"Good," said Adair gratefully. "I wouldn't like to lose that, I can tell you."

"A postage stamp, too, isn't it?" asked Stoodles, looking at it.

"Yes," nodded Adair, "and a pretty valuable one. You see it is canceled and ragged. That don't matter. For all that, the little scrap of paper is worth over two hundred dollars."

"You don't tell me!" gasped Stoodles, staring at the stamp vaguely.

"That's right," insisted Adair. "Here's an island stamp," he added, extending one to Pat. "No, don't bother making change for that trifle. Want to see it?" continued the young man, extending the canceled stamp to Dave.

"I used to have quite a collection myself at home," explained Dave, glancing with interest at the canceled stamp. "Morania? I never heard of that."

"No, a short and solemn history, that of Morania," said Adair. "It was one of the South Sea islands with a population of about one thousand natives. Some shrewd Yankee got their king to establish a post office, so he could sell the government a stamp-printing outfit. There wasn't much business, but one day Morania without any warning was swept to destruction by a tidal wave. Very few letters had ever been sent out. Of course the few stamps to be had became immensely valuable. I have managed to pick up four of them in my travels. I value them at one thousand dollars."

"Why----" said Dave, with a sudden start, and glanced at Stoodles queerly. Whatever the artist's story had suggested, however, Dave did not have time to explain. Captain Broadbeam came storming by like a mad lion.

"There's foul work here," he roared--"foul work all around. First that stupid, drunken pilot runs us afoul of a snag and stove a hole in our bottom. Now that rascally governor sends word asking a small fortune for the timber and truck and men to mend up the Swallow. All right. Pipe the crew, bosun. We'll have to overhaul the keel ourselves and do the best mending we can. Then I'm out of these latitudes mighty quick, I can tell you!"

"Don't he know?" inquired Adair, stepping closer to Dave's side and speaking confidentially.

"Know what?" inquired Dave, in some surprise.

"Why, that the snag he ran into, or rather the snag the pilot ran him into, was a sunken brig that everybody on the island has known for years blocked the creek bottom."

"Is that so?" said Dave.

"As I get it from the talk of the natives here, yes," said Adair.

"Did the pilot know it was there?" asked Dave.

"Could he miss knowing it?" demanded Adair. "Truth is, I came down here with a sort of fellow-feeling in my mind for you people. The governor here and his friends bleed every American they get hold of. They are a precious set of thieves, and when I heard of your predicament I wondered what new mischief they were up to."

"Then," said Dave, in a startled way, "you mean to insinuate that the pilot ran the Swallow into her present fix purposely?"

"I do," nodded Adair.

"Why?" demanded Dave, with a quick catch of excitement in his voice--"why did he do it?"

CHAPTER III

MR. SCHMITT-SCHMITT

"Yes," cried Bob Vilett impulsively. "Why did the pilot try to wreck the Swallow?"

The young engineer had been an interested listener to the conversation that had passed between Dave and Adair. The latter shrugged his shoulders.

"Sheer natural meanness and hatred of foreigners," he said, "or they mean to delay you."

"Why should they delay us?" protested Dave.

"To bleed you. The longer you stay here the more they will get out of you. They overcharge for everything, make you pay, and fine you, and make you trouble on every little technicality of the law that wretched governor can dig up."

"Why, that's abominable!" declared Bob.

"You see, the island here is in a squabble between Chili and Peru," explained the artist. "The governor has set up an independent dictatorship. He knows it can't continue, so he is hurrying to make all the money he can out of his position while it lasts."

"It looks as if you have given us some pretty straight information," said Dave seriously. "I must tell Captain Broadbeam. No," Dave checked himself. "I'll wait till I am sure of what you suspect, and look a little deeper into this matter."

"There's a group I'd like to take," interrupted Adair, glancing with an artist's fine interest at the sailors of the Swallow getting some tackle out to keel the ship.

He seized a boathook and, leaning over the side, caught its end in his camera outfit lying in the skiff below.

"There are some island views, if you would like to look them over," he observed, unstrapping a square portfolio from the camera rack.

Adair set up his portable tripod and focussed the group amidships. Dave turned over the photographs in the portfolio.

"You'll find a pretty good picture of that rascally pilot," said Adair. "Third one, I think."

"I've got it," nodded Dave, "and--say!"

So violent was this ejaculation that Adair was startled into snapping the camera shutter before he was quite ready.

"You've spoiled my picture for me," he said, but not at all crossly. "Why, my friend, what's struck you?"

Dave was wrought up all out of the common. Generally cool and level-headed, his nerves seemed to have suddenly gone to pieces.

He had dropped the portfolio, and Bob was scrambling to preserve its scattered contents. Dave himself held a single photograph in one hand; with the other he was pulling Adair by the arm. He drew the surprised artist out of direct range of the others.

"Look here," he said, with difficulty steadying his trembling voice, "this picture?"

"Yes," nodded Adair, with a casual glance at the photograph--"our friend, the pilot."

"There is no trouble recognizing him," said Dave. "It's the other fellow in the picture, I mean."

"Oh, do you know him?"

"I think I do," answered Dave, in a suppressed but intense tone.

"Likely. He's been haunting the harbors here for several days. I happened to see the two sitting on that bench in front of the pilot's shanty, and took a shot."

Dave, looking worried and hopeful, in doubt and suspicious, by turns, kept scanning the photograph.

"Who is the man, anyhow?" he asked, placing his finger on the pilot's companion.

"Schmitt-Schmitt, he calls himself--from the Dutch West Indies, he says."

"He calls himself that, does he?" said Dave thoughtfully, "and he is a Dutchman?"

"All I know is that he got onto the island here somehow--I believe from a tramp steamer a few days ago. He's close up to the governor and the pilot. Every craft that touches here, he visits its captain and wants to charter the ship."

"He wants to charter a ship," repeated Dave--"what for?"

"Mysterious cruise. He has discovered an island full of diamonds, or a mountain of gold, or some such thing," replied Adair. "He makes fabulous offers to any captain who will take a thirty-day cruise on the speculation. When he turns out all promises and no ready cash, of course the captains laugh at him. Been to you to join in his speculation, eh?"

"No," said Dave emphatically. "He knows too much to try it! Mr. Adair," he continued, warmly grasping the artist's hand, "you have done us a service you little dream of."

"Glad of that," responded Adair, with a hearty smile.

"I don't know how to thank you. May I have this picture for a day or two?"

"Keep it--I've got the negative. Time to go, I fancy," added Adair, as the crew crowded with the repair tackle in their direction.

Dave saw the artist safely into the skiff, waved his hand in adieu, and went in search of his father.

Amos Fearless sat in the cabin, immersed in deep thought.

"What is the captain going to do, father?" asked Dave.

"He's all worked up, and I hardly know how to take him," replied Mr. Fearless. "His only idea for the present is to get away from Minotaur Island; he says they're a set of conscienceless plunderers."

"He is right in that," declared Dave. "Did you suggest to him anything about searching for the stolen gold?"

"I did, Dave."

"What did he say?" eagerly asked Dave.

"He shook his head gloomily, said he would like to help us out, but according to his contract with the owners of the Swallow, he was due in San Francisco. You see, this cruise was taken by him under direction of Doctor Barrell. The doctor having accomplished his mission, there is nothing for him to do but to get the government collection of curiosities home as soon as possible."

Dave looked somewhat cast down at this unfavorable report. Of course, without the Swallow at their service it was useless to think further of the stolen treasure.

"Well, father," he said, after a long, thoughtful spell, "just let things rest as they are for the present. Only I wish you would warn Captain Broadbeam to keep close watch over the Swallow and to allow no strangers aboard."

"Why," exclaimed the old diver, "is there danger?"

"In the air and all around us," declared Dave. "I don't want to alarm you, father, and I don't want to say anything further until I have gone up to the town here."

"Going ashore?" murmured his father, in an uneasy tone. "I wouldn't, Dave, if things are not safe."

"Oh, they will be safe for me, as I shall take Mr. Stoodles and Bob Vilett along with me. When I come back, father, I think I shall have discovered something that will put Captain Broadbeam on his mettle and open the way for one more effort to find the fortune we have been robbed of."

Dave went to the deck again. He sought out Stoodles and Bob in turn and told them he wished them to go to the town with him. Of the trio the young engineer only was under ship discipline. He reported to the boatswain and was soon ready to join the others.

They rowed down the creek to the ocean in a small yawl, rounded the coast, and landed about half a mile from the town.

"I'll just drop my letter to my friends in New York while I'm in town," observed Pat.

"I wouldn't do that if I were you, Mr. Stoodles," advised Dave.

"Eh, why not, lad?" asked Pat.

"Just a few steps further and I will tell you," answered Dave.

He led his companions to a spot where there were some low rocks and motioned them to be seated.

"No one can overhear us at this lonely spot, that is sure," said Dave. "Now then, my friends, I want to have a serious confidential talk with you."

Bob looked curious and Stoodles important.

"Captain Broadbeam is worried and undecided," went on Dave, "my father is slightly discouraged, the crew sullen and discontented over losing that treasure. If no one stirs up something, as we must do--then things will drop, and we will go back home poorer than when we started out. Now, I don't give up so easily."

"Good boy!" nodded Stoodles approvingly.

"I shall make an effort to trace our stolen fortune if I have to do it all alone in a canoe."

"If we only knew where it was," said Bob Vilett. "That's the trouble, you see, Dave. It may be thousands of miles away. It may be adrift on the ocean. It may be halfway to China, or divided up and squandered by that miserable Hankers crowd."

"No," said Dave, with emphasis. "I have pretty good evidence in my possession that the treasure is safe and sound on the Windjammers' Island."

CHAPTER IV

A PAIR OF SCHEMERS

"The treasure is on the Windjammers' Island!" exclaimed Bob Vilett.

"Yes," nodded Dave confidently, "I have every reason to think so."

"Begorra!" cried the Irishman excitedly. "On my paternal dominions? On the principalities of King Patrick Stoodles? A horse, my kingdom for a--no, I mane a ship. Lad, if the goold those Hankers stole is anywhere among my subjects, we'll have it back, mind me!"

"Well, let me explain," said Dave, "and then hear what you have to say. We three have shared too many perils and secrets together, to need to be told that all I tell now is in strict confidence until we get ready to act."

"Spoke like a lawyer," commented Stoodles.

"Like a friend, you mean," corrected Bob. "Leave it to smart Dave to work a way out of a dilemma. I'm interested and excited, Dave."

"Well, first and foremost," continued Dave, "do you recognize that picture, Bob?"

Dave handed out the photograph that Adair had given him on the Swallow.

"Why, sure," answered Bob promptly. "It's a picture of that rascally pilot."

"No, no---I mean the other figure in the photograph."

"Oh--oh!" said Bob slowly, studying it. "N-no," he continued, quite as slowly. "Yes--no. H'm! One minute the face looks familiar, the next it looks strange. I can't fix it, although it seems as if I've seen that man before."

"You have," declared Dave. "Here, Mr. Stoodles, you take a try."

"Yes, there's the pilot," announced Stoodles. "The other is the ould pawnbroker that was on the Raven."

Dave's face grew eager and bright with satisfaction.

"Good for you," he said. "I knew I was right. Yes, that is the man the Hankers picked up at San Francisco--a pawnbroker named Gerstein. He furnished some of the money to fit out their ship for the expedition. Well, my friends, Gerstein, under the false name of Schmitt-Schmitt, is now on this island."

"Then the Raven crowd escaped!" exclaimed Bob.

"I don't know that," answered Dave. "I do know that Schmitt-Schmitt appeared here a few days ago. He has been trying to engage a ship to go after a fortune he says he can find. Of course it's our treasure."

"The spalpane! Of coorse it is!" cried Stoodles excitedly.

"My theory," went on Dave, "is that the Raven was terribly disabled or lost in the cyclone. I am also pretty sure that the treasure was saved. Perhaps it was already hidden somewhere on land. At all events, Schmitt-Schmitt was in the secret, either as the partner and emissary of others of the Raven crowd or on his own account. He managed to get a small boat afloat, was taken up by a liner, and landed here. Now his whole time is given, as I said, to finding a ship that will go after a fortune, as he terms it, on shares."

"Your theory is raisonable, your theory is right," insisted Stoodles.

"Schmitt-Schmitt," proceeded Dave, "made friends with the governor here. He seems to be staying at the pilot's house. When the Swallow was sighted he at once reasoned it out that we had discovered the real contents of those four boxes, that we might be bound straight back for the Windjammers' Island. He induced the pilot to run us onto the sunken brig in the creek."

"Dave, I believe you've got this matter just right," said Bob thoughtfully.

"If that is true," continued Dave, "they will do all they can to delay us. Who knows but what this rascally governor and his crew may intend to take the Swallow away from us and furnish Schmitt-Schmitt with the very means he wants to go after the treasure, with no chance of being followed?"

"Dave, have you told Captain Broadbeam about all this?" inquired Bob anxiously.

"I haven't had the chance. I learned what I have told you only in the past hour," responded Dave. "As soon as we return to the Swallow, though, I shall warn him. I had a purpose in coming ashore."

"Are we to help you, Dave?" asked Bob.

"All hands must help. I want to locate the pilot's house, I want to be sure that this Schmitt-Schmitt is really there and that he is the same fellow we knew as Gerstein on the Raven."

"That's easy," declared Stoodles. "The picture gives us a hint as to the house."

"We will separate so as to excite no notice or suspicions," directed Dave. "Let each one of us find out all he can, and report at this spot in three hours."

"In three hours be it," nodded Stoodles, looking very businesslike.

"All right," assented Bob, taking another good look at the picture of the pilot's house.

Dave allowed his two friends to select their own course. Then, when they were out of sight, he took an independent route.

He surmised that the pilot would probably live near the water's edge. In this he found his calculations correct, and an hour's search brought some results.

"That is the house," spoke Dave finally, peering from a clump of thick high bushes. "Yes, there is the very bench the pilot and Schmitt-Schmitt sat on when Mr. Adair took their picture."

Before Dave lay a ground plot of considerable extent and fairly smothered in luxurious vegetation, sloping down to the beach. In its center was a lone hut, open and rambling, and having a broad porch that ran clear around it.

It was a typical tropical habitation of the poorer class. No one seemed stirring about the place except far back in the rear. Here there was a thick plantation of high resinous bushes. One man was feeding these into a rude grinding mill operated by a big lazy mule treading in a circle.

Dave stood quietly in his place of concealment for fully half an hour. The man drove his mule away. The place seemed now entirely deserted. However, just as Dave was about to leave the spot someone came out on the front porch.

"It's the man. Yes, sure, it is Gerstein--Schmitt-Schmitt!" said Dave.

Schmitt-Schmitt was dressed in a thin linen suit. He carried a large but light wicker valise. This he set down beside a bench, looked at his watch, then in the direction of the town, and stretched himself out lazily in a hammock.

"Looks as if he was going away," mused Dave, critically analyzing all the movements of the person he was spying on. "Looks too as if he was expecting and waiting for somebody--probably the pilot."

Dave thought out the situation and its possibilities for about five minutes. He decided to go back to the yawl. Then he realized that he would be considerably interested in hearing what the pilot and his guest might say when they met.

Schmitt-Schmitt lay with his back to Dave. On this account, and because of the shelter of many shrubs and bushes, Dave found it no task at all to cover the space unnoticed between his present hiding-place and the porch.

Its floor was nearly two feet from the ground. Dave crawled way back under this open space, got pretty nearly under the hammock, and lay on his back. The porch boards were badly warped and splintered, and he could look right up at the hammock and its occupant.

At the end of about ten minutes Dave heard footsteps coming up the graveled walk. He turned his eyes sideways and was gratified to recognize the pilot.

"Whew, this is hot!" ejaculated the owner of the place, stamping heavily across the porch and throwing himself into a chair near the hammock, in which Schmitt-Schmitt now arose to a sitting posture. Then the speaker glanced in the direction of the plantation where Dave had noticed the treadmill.

"Ah," continued the pilot, with an angry scowl. "That lazy rascal has ceased making the frew-frew? I will cut him half a day's pay."

"Yes, it is hot," answered his guest. Each of the precious twain had a language of his own, so they compromised on very broken English.

"What you done?" asked Schmitt-Schmitt. The pilot chuckled and grinned from ear to ear.

"I have undone," he said gleefully. "Have I not? But the governor went too far. He charged them prices for repairing the Swallow the captain wouldn't stand, and he is doing his own repairing."

"He is?" cried Schmitt-Schmitt, in a tone of alarm. "He is quick, smart. He will be off in twenty-four hours."

"Not at all," declared the pilot calmly. "You wish him delayed? Delay it shall be, a long delay. Delay after delay. Only--my pay must come. The governor's too. We are exceeding the law for you."

"Both of you shall be rich--rich! As soon as I get my fortune," promised Schmitt-Schmitt recklessly. "Have you found out for me yet--do they think they have the treasure aboard the Swallow?"

"They have just found out differently, my spies tell me," said the pilot.

"Then they will go right back to search for it," declared Schmitt-Schmitt. "I know them--plucky fellows, all. They must be stopped."

"Fear not. As I told you," interrupted the pilot calmly, "that end of it is easy. I hope your getting the treasure is as simple."

"Get these fellows out of the way, get me a ship, and I will show you," said Schmitt-Schmitt eagerly.

"One thing at a time, then," Dave heard the pilot say next in order. "See, my friend."

"A brush, a little bottle of paint?" inquired Schmitt-Schmitt.

Dave wriggled and twisted his neck to get a focus on these two articles, which the pilot held up. Then the pilot leaned over and said something to his companion in so low a tone that Dave could not catch its import.

"Capital, capital, oh, that is just famous!" gloated Schmitt-Schmitt. "You have found the man to experiment on?"

"He will be here to-night."

"And after the stuff is on?"

"Bah--a sponge and some turpentine, and the patient recovers."

"Good, good!" said Schmitt-Schmitt. "Yes, that will indeed delay the Swallow. Now, listen, my friend: I must not run the risk of being seen by any of the Swallow people."

"No, indeed."

"It would at once give them their cue--my escape from the Windjammers' Island. I have packed my valise, I will disappear for a few days."

"Excellent. You will go at once?"

"I think so. You will remember! A blue light, I am sick or in danger. A red light, I need provisions."

"Signal any time from ten to twelve. I will be on the watch. If you say so I will start up the launch at once and take you to your destination."

"H'm," mused Dave, as double footsteps sounded the length of the porch. "Some new mysterious trick to delay the Swallow? Schmitt-Schmitt going away somewhere? This is too interesting to miss."

Dave crept out from under the porch. He dodged in among some bushes. Peering thence he saw Schmitt-Schmitt leading the way towards the beach, the pilot carrying his wicker satchel.

Dave did not venture to follow them direct. He lined the "frew-frew" plantation, and at a clearing in it near the treadmill cut across it.

From the grinding-mill a rude wooden trough extended. This was full of a sticky resinous mass, and the ground all round was spattered with the glutinous substance.

"Frew-frew must be a sort of gum or oil they make from those stalks yonder," decided Dave. "The mischief! it's worse than fly paper."

Dave's shoes stuck to broad leaves and lifted them bodily as he walked; they became tangled in vines which raised about him like ropes. He made an effort to get out of the direct zone of stickiness.

Dave leaped over the edge of a board where the wooden trough ran in among tangled vines and plants.

"Oh, yes!" he gasped. In an instant, as his feet struck a soft, giving mass, Dave knew he was in danger. Unconsciously he had landed in the center of an immense cistern--the storage receptacle for the frew-frew product.

He tried to reach its edge but was held fast. He struggled to release his limbs but was pulled back and dragged down.

Dave sank in five seconds to the neck. His chin went under. As he started to yell his mouth was submerged. With a last dip eyesight was shut out and Dave sank under the sticky mass entirely submerged.

CHAPTER V

DOCTOR BARRELL'S "ACCIDENT"

"Begorra!"

That was the first expressive word that Dave Fearless heard as he realized that he had been suddenly saved from death by suffocation.

His eyes, mouth, ears, and nostrils were oozing with the sticky stuff in which he had taken so dangerous a bath. The top of his head seemed coming off. Dave felt as if he had been scalped.

Dave was lying on the grass and Stoodles was working over him, digging and dabbling with a handkerchief to get the youth's eyes and mouth clear of the glutinous "frew-frew."

"Sorra a bit too soon was I," said Pat, as Dave blinked and groaned. "I've a lock of your hair for a keepsake, lad! I saw you go into that threacherous pit, I threw a plank across, I grasped your topknot. It was loike taking a drowned cat out of glue. Sit up, if you can't stand up. If you let that stuff harden once, you'll be stiff as a statoo."

Dave tried to arise. He dragged grass, dirt, vines, and weeds up with him. By this time he could breathe and see. Stoodles got a stick and scraped off from his clothes as much as he could of the adhesive mass that coated Dave.

"Come on, lad," directed Stoodles, grasping an arm of his tottering companion. "It's a brickdust bath in soft soap you'll be needing. Acushla! but I stick to you like a brother."

Dave's feet gathered up everything they came in contact with. Then, every time he brushed a bit of foliage, the frew-frew took off leaves, and he began to look green and picturesque.

"Where is Bob Vilett?" he asked.

"I dunno," answered Stoodles. "I do know it was lucky I saw you thrailing the pilot and that rascally pawnbroker. If I hadn't you'd have been a goner, Dave Fearless."

"I guess I should," responded Dave, with a shudder, and then a grateful look at this eccentric but loyal friend. "Where have those two gone--did you notice, Mr. Stoodles?"

"Only that they set off seaward in a little launch."

"Get me to the Swallow, I have a lot to tell Captain Broadbeam now."

They lined the beach. A good many craft of various kinds were visible in the opening. All of them were too far distant to enable Dave to make out which one might contain the pilot and Schmitt-Schmitt.

When they got to the place of rendezvous where they had left the ship's yawl, Bob Vilett was discovered lying on the sand.

"Wandered off on a wrong trail," he reported; "wasted time and thought I was due here. Dave, what have you been into!"

"Frew-frew, I believe they call it, Bob."

"Phew-phew I'd call it," remarked Pat. "Up with the jibboom and across the briny, Bob. If we don't get our friend Fearless into hot water and soap soon, we'll have to chip off his coat of mail with chisels."

When they reached the Swallow they found the steamer the center of vast bustle and industry. Captain Broadbeam had keeled the craft and gangs of men were working inside and outside to repair the breaks in the hull.

The cabins and forecastle were accessible, but Mike Conners had temporarily removed cooking headquarters to a tent at the side of the creek. Stoodles sought out Mr. Drake, the boatswain, and explained Dave's dilemma. They rigged up a canvas bathroom on shore and supplied it with brushes, two tubs of boiling suds, and plenty of soap.

It took Dave over an hour to get off the worst of the villainous frew-frew. His hair was the hardest to clean. Finally he emerged, fresh and tingling in every nerve from the vigorous bath.

They had supper ashore and hammocks were rigged up under the trees. Captain Broadbeam set a guard about camp and ship. About half the crew decided to quit and he paid them off. They and curious visitors from the town were warned to keep away from the Swallow.

About dusk Captain Broadbeam had given out all necessary orders for the night.

"Well, lad," he said, coming up to Dave and placing his hand on the youth's shoulder in his usually friendly way, "I understand you have something important to tell me."

"Yes, considerable," answered Dave.

"All right. The others interested must hear it, too. We'll hold a council of war in my cabin."

Dave's father, Doctor Barrell, Stoodles, and Bob Vilett were invited to accompany the captain and Dave to the Swallow. The six of them soon found themselves seated in the captain's cabin. It slanted slightly from the present awkward position of the ship, but they managed to adjust the stools and settees comfortably.

"Now then, lad," spoke Captain Broadbeam to Dave, "my old friend here, your father, has intimated to me that you have discovered some things of general interest to all of us."

"I think I have," said Dave.

"Then fire away, my hearty."

Dave began his story with a narration of the visit to the Swallow of the young artist Adair. He followed this up with his discovery of Schmitt-Schmitt, and his overhearing of the conversation between that worthy and the treacherous native pilot.

Captain Broadbeam was interested from the first; when it became apparent from Dave's clear, logical story that the stolen treasure was still somewhere in the vicinity of the Windjammers' Island, the old tar's eyes glistened and he looked eager and excited. Then, as Dave told of the evident existence of a plot to delay, possibly destroy, the Swallow, Captain Broadbeam sprang to his feet.

"Delay me, will they?" he shouted, growing red of face and blazing with anger. "Why, the miserable scum! if they so much as hang around here I'll fill them with a charge of pepper and salt. If I catch them up to any tricks aboard, I'll swing them from the yardarm."

The doughty old mariner paced the cabin in a fine rage. When he had subsided Dave approached the subject nearest his thoughts.

"Captain," he began, "from what I have told don't you really think my theories are right as to the treasure being hidden?"

"I do, lad, I'll admit that," growled the captain.

"And that this fellow Schmitt-Schmitt is an emissary of the Hankers and the Raven, looking for a ship to go after the treasure?"

"Mebbe, lad, mebbe."

"Then what is the matter with hurrying up your repairs and getting back to the Windjammers' Island before Schmitt-Schmitt? Don't you see, captain, we are bound to locate the Raven crew, if they are there?"

Captain Broadbeam sank to a stool, bent his head, and groaned.

"Lad," he said, "I know what you want to do and what I'd like to do. It can't be done--no, no."

"Captain," interrupted Amos Fearless, in an eager, quivering tone, "we are old friends----"

"Belay there!" roared the veteran tar, springing to his feet and waving his ponderous arms like windmills. "Would ye tempt a man from his duty who has never yet over-stepped discipline? That duty is plain, Amos Fearless. This here Swallow was sent out to collect curiosities for the United States Government. Those curiosities are duly collected. Incidentally I helped you fellows all I could on the side. Now it's San Francisco. Them's my sailing orders. There's my duty."

"Ochone!" groaned Pat Stoodles, "and phwat of the foine treasure?"

"I'm out of this hornets' nest here the minute the Swallow is seaworthy," announced Broadbeam. "The minute I land at San Francisco and get my clearance, I'll hark back to the Windjammers with you if I have to put all my savings into chartering a ship specially."

"It will be too late then, captain," murmured Dave, in a dejected tone.

"Sorry," said the commander of the Swallow. "I am responsible to the owners. Why, friends, if I should step outside of my duty I am personally liable to a fine that would make me a ruined man and a pauper."

Dave gave a queer start at this, a quick color came into his cheek, a quick flicker into his eyes. He gazed at Stoodles in an eager, speculative way.

"One moment, captain, please," he said, arising and beckoning Stoodles to follow him from the cabin, "I have just thought of something important. I hope you will not decide finally on this matter until I have had a word in private with Mr. Stoodles."

"Surely not, lad," nodded the captain, but in some wonder regarding this peculiar move on the part of the young fellow he had grown to like greatly.

Silence fell over the little coterie in the cabin then. They could hear the low hum of voices outside; Dave talking rapidly and earnestly, and such violent ejaculations from Stoodles now and then as "Begorra!" "Luk at that now!" "Bedad!" and the like.

When Dave came back into the cabin he was calm and collected, but Stoodles squirmed about with a wise, important look on his moonlike face.

"Captain Broadbeam," said Dave, "I have just consulted with Mr. Stoodles on a matter covering his ability to raise a certain sum of money."

The captain of the Swallow grinned. It was so ridiculous to think of Stoodles ever earning or saving a penny that he could not well help it.

"Yes," announced Pat gravely, "by my royal authority as king of the Windjammers' Island."

"Nonsense," muttered Captain Broadbeam.

"You will take my word for it, captain, won't you?" insinuated Dave, in his smooth, convincing way. "I can say to you positively that if you will land Mr. Stoodles among his former subjects for a single hour, and later safely at San

Francisco, he will be prepared to pay you five thousand dollars to meet any fines the owners of the Swallow may assess you for going back there."

"Why, Dave," began Mr. Fearless in wonderment--but Bob Vilett interrupted.

"If Dave says five thousand dollars, he means five thousand dollars."

"Remarkable!" commented Doctor Barrell, surveying Dave in astonishment through his eyeglasses close-set.

Captain Broadbeam was impressed. He studied Dave and Stoodles speculatively.

"How can you possibly get that sum of money?" he demanded.

"We can," declared Dave positively, "can't we, Mr. Stoodles?"

"Begorra! and ten if we nade it!" cried Pat enthusiastically. "Oh, the broth of a boy! It takes my friend Dave Fearless for brains."

"Of course it is a secret," said Dave.

"A deadly saycret--I mane a close one," declared Stoodles. "I never knew how rich I was till the lad told me just now."

"Oh, pshaw!" exclaimed Captain Broadbeam, dismissing the matter with a worried motion of his hand. "Money can't count in this case. My duty is plain! I was ordered to sail for the home port as soon as the government collection was made. Doctor Barrell reported a month ago that he had finished that collection."

"H'm, just so," observed Doctor Barrell, "but, my dear sir--ha, a thought. A moment, Captain Broadbeam, just a moment."

"Thunder!" whistled Bob Vilett amazedly in his chum's ear. "What does that mean now?"

Dave shook his head in silent wonderment. Doctor Barrell had winked at them in a quizzical, encouraging way that was mightily suggestive.

To have the high-class old scientist so far forget his dignity was a most remarkable thing.

They heard Doctor Barrell stumbling about in the aft cabin where he had stored some of the curiosities he had gathered for the government.

Suddenly there was a loud bump followed by a great clash. The next minute the doctor burst into the captain's cabin holding aloft two cracked and broken specimens of starfish.

"Captain," he cried--"bad accident! The collection is incomplete. See, Captain Broadbeam, the only specimens of the Mercuria stellaticus we had, destroyed, case tipped over."

The commander of the Swallow bestowed a searching look on the speaker, but was silent. "They are to be found only at the Windjammers' Island," went on Doctor Barrell. "Oh, dear, dear! This will, I fear, necessitate a return to the island."

"Oh, will it?" snorted the captain sarcastically. "So, you're in the plot, too, to lure me from my duty, hey, you old conspirator? Well, you mutinous old humbug, after breaking your mercurian stellians purposely, you'll not get me to go a single knot back on the west course till you sign a paper officially ordering me to do so as a necessity of the expedition."

"Pen and ink--quick," chuckled Doctor Barrell. "Captain," he added pathetically, indicating their sturdy, loyal companions with a kindly affectionate wave of his hand, "their hearts are set on that stolen treasure, rightly too. They are our true, good friends. Honestly, won't you be glad to help them try and find it?"

"Shiver my timbers, but you're a set of conspiring mutineers!" roared the captain doughtily, but the fierce words were spoken with a secret chuckle.

CHAPTER VI

THE PILOT'S PLOT

"Hurrah!" shouted Bob Vilett, tossing his cap up in the air.

"Don't crow too quickly, Bob," warned Dave Fearless. "We're not out of the woods yet."

"And don't you croak," retorted the sprightly young engineer of the Swallow. "Captain Broadbeam says that by this time to-morrow we will be on our way to the Windjammers' Island."

"Yes," nodded Dave significantly, "provided they let us start."

"Eh, who?" demanded Bob.

"The governor here and the pilot, Schmitt-Schmitt, the whole crowd, who I am persuaded are in league to delay us."

"Oh, nonsense," cried Bob airily. "What right have they to interfere with our business?"

"What right had they to wreck the Swallow?" inquired Dave pertinently. "I don't say they will dare to try to make us any further trouble, but they have planned to, that I know, and every one of us must keep our eyes wide open until we leave Minotaur Island far to the rear."

For all Dave's misgivings, however, he was a happy, hopeful boy. It had been settled that they should return to the Windjammers' Island to secure duplicates of the Mercuria stellaticus which Doctor Barrell had disposed of by accident.

"The royal old trump!" Bob Vilett had enthused. "Good-by to that treasure if the doctor hadn't acted so promptly. But I say, Dave, what was that bluff you and Stoodles worked up about five thousand dollars?"

"No bluff at all, as you call it," declared Dave seriously. "A hint from that artist Adair gave me a fine suggestion. Stoodles can easily make five, ten, yes, maybe twenty thousand dollars if he has a chance to once more, even for a single hour, regain his position as king of the Windjammers."

"If I didn't know you so well, Dave Fearless," said Bob gravely, "I'd say you was romancing."

"Wait till you see the reality, Bob," advised Dave, with a confident smile. "By the way, about this same secret of Stoodles'--I must make some purchases in the town to-day."

Just after noon, in pursuance with this suggestion, Dave was rowed to the town by the boatswain and two others of the crew of the Swallow.

When he returned he carried two heavy boxes, storing them safely under lock and key in the purser's own closet.

The inquisitive Bob tried to pump Stoodles, but it was of no avail. Pat looked crafty and wise, and only muttered some remarks about his royal prerogative and the like.

By sundown the Swallow had been completely repaired. She was righted and cleaned up, and everything put in order for a run to Mercury Island. Captain Broadbeam decided to provision up there. He was uneasy every minute he dallied among the tricky inhabitants of Minotaur Island.

They were short-handed as to a crew, on account of the desertions of the day previous. Several natives had applied for work, but the captain was distrustful of them as spies.

The second mate had several times gone to the main harbor port in search of English sailors, but there chanced to be none unemployed just then. He did manage, however, to pick up one recruit. This was a sickly-looking white man who called himself Tompkins. He was quiet and industrious, and wanted to go as far as Mercury Island, he said to the captain, who entered him regularly on the crew's list.

There had been a great ado that afternoon over maps, charts, and other details pertaining to a long cruise. Captain Broadbeam had engaged Dave in conversation several times about his discoveries and theories.

Both the captain and Amos Fearless now believed that Dave had reasoned out matters concerning the stolen treasure just as they existed in fact.

They could not hope to gain any specific information from Schmitt-Schmitt, even if they learned where he was now keeping himself in seclusion.

"No," Captain Broadbeam had concluded, "we won't stir up affairs any further hereabouts. We will let the people here believe that we are going home to the United States. Schmitt-Schmitt never dreams that we know of his living here. His suspicions will be allayed. We shall leave a clear field and probably get to the Windjammers' Island before he even finds a ship to go in search of the treasure."

The camp on shore was now broken up and its temporary equipment moved back to the Swallow. The work on the steamer was all in shipshape order by supper time. The men had labored diligently, and the captain ordered an extra-fine meal.

It was an hour of typical comfort. A brisk breeze had cooled the air, the sky was bright and clear, the surroundings picturesque and beautiful.

Some of the sailors were singing a jaunty rollicking sea ditty. Dave and Bob paced the after-deck full of their plans for the prospective voyage to begin on the morrow.

"This is certainly life as she is on the ocean wave," declared Bob enthusiastically.

"I love the smell of the brine, Bob," said Dave. "I was born breathing it, and now the seafaring life seems to be a regular business proposition with me."

"Good business, if you recover all that money," observed Bob.

"Look there, Bob," spoke Dave suddenly.

His companion turned. Facing the coast end of the creek a gruesome-looking craft with black funnels, and odd and awkward of shape, was hovering about the mouth of the little inlet.

"Hello," exclaimed Bob, "that's the government ironclad. What's she doing here?"

"Yes," nodded Dave, taking up a telescope and looking through it, "that's the Chili, the governor's special warship, sure. They say she's a poor apology of a craft. Bought her second-hand from some English shipyard. They are putting off a yawl."

"Going to visit us?" inquired Bob.

"It looks that way."

"More trouble?" insinuated Bob.

"More meddling and spying, more like," said Dave.

Both boys watched a natty, well-manned yawl come spinning up the creek towards the Swallow.

The Chilian colors adorned the bow, indicating an official visit. A man in military dress directed the boat. Beside him sat another of the governor's aides in semi-official uniform.

Dave called Captain Broadbeam, and all hands on board the Swallow were now interested in the approaching yawl.

"Colonel José Silverado, from his excellency the governor," announced the officer in charge of the yawl as he neared the side of the steamer.

"Coming aboard?" asked Broadbeam, in his blunt, gruff way.

"On duty, yes," responded the officer, very politely, but with a covert grin. "The governor's physician--Dr. Monterey," added the officer, indicating his companion.

Captain Broadbeam bowed brusquely, and with surly and suspicious mien awaited the further pleasure of the governor's envoy.

The officer glanced keenly all about the ship. Then he took a card from his pocket and scanned it.

"Sorry to trouble you, captain," he said, "but we have reason to believe that you have a refugee aboard your ship."

"A refugee?" repeated Broadbeam, with a start. "Who is he?"

"Man named Tompkins."

"Why, yes," admitted the captain, "we have a new man here by that name."

"Will you kindly summon him? We have business with him. That is the man, doctor?" inquired the officer, as the sickly-looking fellow employed by the Swallow that morning slipped out from among the crew at a call from Captain Broadbeam.

"Ah, yes," nodded the governor's physician, eying Tompkins critically. "My man, you are making us a whole heap of trouble, it seems."

Tompkins looked confused and ill at ease, gazing surlily at the deck.

"What's the matter with him?" demanded the captain.

"Suspect," announced the officer quickly. "Came in on a fruit boat a few days ago. Boat infected, and this man and the others put in quarantine. He got away. Look him over, doctor."

Monterey stepped up to Tompkins. He examined his pulse and his tongue and tapped him on the chest. Then he said tersely:

"Strip."

Tompkins pulled off his shirt. As his naked back came into view several of the crew curiously regarding the scene uttered quick, startled exclamations.

Across the chest, shoulders, and arms of the suspect, the refugee, were half-a-hundred purple-black blotches.

"Spotted fever," said the governor's physician, stepping back as if his task was done and over with.

"Tut! tut! Too bad," observed Silverado. "Captain, I regret to say that this is a quarantine case."

"Eh? Oh, just so," responded Broadbeam. "Well, take him to the pesthouse, then."

The officer shook his head slowly.

"Gone too far for that," he said. "He has probably infected the others. Let no man leave the ship," he called out loudly to some of the crew who were moving away in the haste of fright. "I declare this ship in a state of quarantine," pursued Silverado, in a tone of command, producing a document bearing an official red seal. "We will send you a yellow flag, captain, and you will remain here subject to official orders."

"Quarantined?" cried the captain, bristling up. "And for spotted fever? See here, colonel, we have a skilled physician on board. We will move out to sea at once and take our own risk on this matter."

"Impossible," dissented Silverado, smiling sweetly, but with the latent malice of triumph in his undertone. "Law of the nations--no right to imperil the general safety. No, within two weeks we will give you clearance if no new cases break out. Meantime----"

The officer coolly affixed the sealed document in his hand to the mainmast.

Captain Broadbeam wriggled, fumed, groaned. He was too thorough a seaman to mistake his predicament. His brow grew dark and threatening.

"Bob, quick, come here."

With a violent jerk Dave Fearless pulled his startled chum to one side.

"Quick as you can," he spoke rapidly, "rush to the purser. Tell him to instantly send me up a rag that has been well saturated in turpentine."

"Why, Dave----"

"No questions, no delay," ordered Dave peremptorily.

Bob shot away on his mission, Dave set his teeth, breathing hard. In a flash a sinister suspicion had arisen in his mind. Like lightning memory flew back to the overheard interview on the porch of the native pilot between that crafty individual and the tricky Schmitt-Schmitt.

"He said he could delay the Swallow, he hinted at spots, some paint, at washing them off," mused Dave. "Good for you. Hold on."

Dave snatched the rag soaked with turpentine from Bob Vilett's hands. He ran forward now to where his friends were depressedly watching Tompkins arranging his shirt to replace it.

Dave made a dash at the man. He held him firmly by one shoulder. With his free hand he slapped the rag briskly over his bare flesh to and fro.

Dave's eyes sparkled immediately with the intensest satisfaction. One by one the dark spots on the back of Tompkins began to disappear.

"Captain Broadbeam," cried Dave, pulling the squirming Tompkins around into full view, "a paint-trick. This man has got no more spotted fever than I have myself."

CHAPTER VII

THE MYSTERIOUS JAR

Dave Fearless had saved the day. The young ocean diver knew this the moment he glanced at the faces of those about him.

The wretch Tompkins shrank and cowered in a guilty manner. The squeamish crew looked relieved. The governor's physician and his military companion affected a profound astonishment, but secretly were overwhelmed with confusion and chagrin.

Captain Broadbeam's eyes opened wide in amazement at the first. Then as he guessed it out that a plot against him had been attempted they blazed with wrath.

"Put that man in irons," he roared out.

"Pardon, captain," interrupted Silverado, stepping forward, "we will do that. There is some grave mistake here."

"Mistake?" shouted Broadbeam. "Villainy, a conspiracy. Why----"

"The governor will investigate this matter thoroughly," said Silverado.

Dave had glided to the captain's side. In a quick undertone he advised him to smother his wrath for policy's sake. They allowed their visitors to hustle Tompkins into their boat. To the last Silverado wore a suave mask of forced politeness.

"You vile scum," broke out Broadbeam, shaking his fist after the departing yawl. "It's hard to keep the bit between my teeth and say nothing when I know that all hands from the governor down are in this dirty plot."

The old salt bestowed an approving look on Dave and hustled to the forecastle, calling the crew around him.

"Dave, how did you ever come to think of it?" marveled Bob Vilett.

"Why, it was simple--putting two and two together. I remembered the pilot's talk about paint," replied Dave. "Hear that! Captain Broadbeam is on his mettle."

Both boys listened to the sonorous voice of the commander of the Swallow. He was greatly aroused. They heard him give orders to have the entire armament of the Swallow put in active commission. A stand of rifles was to be set ready for use. To Mr. Drake was delegated the task of furbishing up two old brass ten-pounders from the hold.

"We sail to-morrow," announced the captain. "Look out for tricks to-night. These villains won't let us go without meddling further if they can help it.

My men, I ask you all to stand by me if there's a scrimmage, and there will be one if those fellows try to block my way."

Dave came in for a good deal of attention from the captain, Doctor Barrell, and his father, when affairs had quieted down somewhat. They all realized that his good memory and shrewd forethought had saved them a vexatious delay and no end of further trouble from the treacherous governor and his cohorts.

"I will be glad when we get clear of the island to-morrow," said Dave, as Bob turned in for the night.

It had been a busy, exciting day, and Dave was glad to have a few moments to himself to think over affairs in general.

He stretched himself on a heap of canvas in the shadow of the rear cabin, overlooking the creek and the beautiful moonlit expanse stretching out beyond it.

Dave mused, dozed, woke up, and stretched himself. He heard the night-watch laughing and talking in low tones amidships.

"I'll join them, listen to one or two of their wild yarns, and then turn in for the night myself," he decided.

Half-arising, however, Dave came to a rigid pose. He stared hard beyond the rail and down into the still waters of the creek.

Everything was so calm and still that the least sound or movement was vividly distinct to ear and eye.

Dave's eye had detected a ripple in the quiet waters. Then momentarily a human head had protruded into view.

It bobbed down under water again. It came up ten feet nearer to the Swallow. It disappeared once more, and this seemed to carry it past the watcher's direct range of vision.

"Someone, and up to something," declared Dave to himself. "Hark, now."

He bent his ear keenly. A soft drip-drip sounded just beyond the rail. Then a black hand glistening with water clutched the rail itself.

Slowly, cautiously the body of a dusky native, attired only in swimming garb, came into view. This was the person Dave had detected swimming under water.

Straddling the rail, the intruder crouched, looking all about the deck. Then he lifted both feet over onto the planking.

Dave now noticed that the man carried under one arm quite a bulky package done up in black oilskin.

The intruder glanced sharply at the forecastle. Just abutting it was a box-like section into which all kinds of odds and ends of canvas and ropes were bundled. Its door was half-ajar. Dave saw the stranger glide to this, thrust his package inside, glide back to the rail, slip over it, and drop into the water.

A minute later the ripples in the creek showed where the fellow was making his retreat under water. His head came up to the surface once or twice. Then he arose at a distance down the stream and disappeared among the dense shrubbery lining the creek.

"More mischief," instantly decided Dave Fearless.

Dave made a rush for the forecastle cubby hole. He pulled its door wide open and groped about. His fingers closed about a dripping object there.

"Hard and heavy," said Dave. "Wrapped in the oilskin to protect it. What can it be?"

Dave arose to his feet. Suddenly a thrill passed through his frame.

"Put here for a purpose," he thought. "Can it be an explosive!"

Internally Dave became immensely excited. Coolly, however, though carrying the dubious object as though it were an egg, he proceeded to the ship's rail nearest the shore.

Dave set the object gently on the rail, climbed over, took it up again, and, holding it above his head in one hand, dropped into the water.

The splash, slight as it was, aroused the watch. Two men came hurrying to the rail.

"Hold on, there," challenged one of them.

"It's only me--Dave Fearless," came the retort promptly, "cooling off--a little swim, that's all."

"You pick a fine time for it."

Dave laughed. He liked water, and swam with one hand, came ashore, and went past its fringe of brush to a clearing.

"Now then," said Dave, with a great sigh of relief, at a safe distance from the ship, "burst, if you want to!"

Dave had set the object he carried down on the ground. He stepped back a few feet and survcyed it suspiciously.

"A bomb?" he questioned himself. "How am I going to find out? Perhaps it's some infernal machine loaded with phosphorus. Then those villains intended to burn the Swallow. Certainly this means some black mischief."

Dave roamed about till he found a stout long reed. Then he began to poke at the object he had brought from the ship. He finally managed to remove its oilskin covering.

"It's a jar, a stone jar," he said, "queer and foreign-looking, like we get snuff or preserved ginger in. Labeled, too, and seals across the top. It don't look very dangerous, for all the sinister way it came aboard."

Dave did not belie his name. He dallied with the situation no longer and now took up the jar fearlessly.

Its label resembled the covering used on a package of firecrackers. The seal was of tin-foil stamped with similar characters in red.

"Chinese, that's sure," thought Dave. "Shall I risk it?" he questioned himself, his fingers surrounding the jar cover.

Dave snapped the seal and removed the cover. A layer of tissue paper showed. He pulled this out. A dense stench was emitted by the jar. He poked his finger down into the contents. They were solid and sticky.

"Why," said Dave, a good deal puzzled, sniffing vigorously, "it's opium."

CHAPTER VIII

OUTWITTING AN ENEMY

Dave Fearless stood looking over the queer jar and its contents very thoughtfully.

"Well," he declared at length, "this is a puzzle."

Under ordinary circumstances Dave might have supposed that some sailor addicted to the use of opium had hired some emissary to smuggle some of the drug aboard ship.

This, however, did not look rational in the present case. In the first place the contents of the jar represented over a year's pay of the average sailor. In the next place it was too easy to get it aboard by ordinary methods to occasion all this mystery.

Of course Dave at once decided that the placing of the opium in the forecastle cubby-hole was part and parcel of the same plot that had nearly wrecked the Swallow, that later just that day had developed the unsuccessful attempt at quarantining the steamer.

"What's the motive in this latest trick?" mused Dave. "Aha!" he exclaimed suddenly, "have I guessed it right?"

A quick suspicion, a prompt suggestion came to Dave's mind. He was speedy to act.

"I think I've struck the clew," he said--"I think I'm acting right in this matter."

Dave, carrying the jar with him, wandered about till he found a decayed tree stump. He emptied the opium into a hole in the wood and covered it over with bark.

Dave scraped the jar and made a little ball of the leavings, a sample of the stuff he might need for later experience and evidence.

This he did up in a piece of paper, shoving it in a safe pocket. He washed out the jar thoroughly. Then he wandered about studying the branches of various trees under which he passed. Several of these Dave ascended like a boy bird's-nesting.

He was quite a long time in one tree-top. When he descended to the ground he had the cover firmly attached to the jar, which he carried as if extremely careful of its contents.

"If I am guessing things out right," said Dave, with a kind of satisfied chuckle, "I think we shall give our enemies quite a novel surprise."

Dave swam back to the steamer. Arrived on deck he placed the jar just where he had originally found it. Then he went to bed.

He overslept himself next morning. The ship was a scene of bustle and activity. When he came up on deck, every member of the crew proper was busy, even Bob Vilett.

So Dave found no opportunity to make a confidant of his special chum, even had that been his desire or intention.

At nine o'clock Captain Broadbeam announced that all was ready for their departure, and ordered steam up.

Within thirty minutes of getting under way the boatswain hurried from the bow to where the captain was standing amidships.

"Coming again, sir," he announced, touching the peak of his cap respectfully.

"Who's coming?" demanded Broadbeam.

"Those buzzards--same gang in the longboat that was here last night."

"Humph!" growled the captain, gazing stormily at a yawl just rounded from open water into the mouth of the creek.

The approaching craft was directed by the plausible Silverado. Smiling as ever he came on board, three men with him.

"From his excellency the governor," he said.

"Yes, yes," answered Captain Broadbeam crossly; "I know all that rigmarole. What do you want?"

"A complaint, captain."

"Who from?"

"I do not know."

"What about?"

"Contraband goods--smuggling."

Captain Broadbeam laughed in the officer's face outright.

"Guess not," he said. "I reckon, my friend, about all we will take away from Minotaur Island will be a mighty poor opinion of its inhabitants."

"Oh, I trust not," the polite official hastened to say, but added tersely: "We must make a search."

"What for?"

"I have told you--contraband goods. We are having a good deal of trouble in this line. Ships touching here make the island a sort of clearing house for dutiable imports and exports. Our governor's high sense of honor demands extreme vigilance and discipline. We are authorized to make a search."

"Search away," cried Broadbeam indifferently, but with some show of mental irritation.

Silverado and his aids went into the hold. They made a great pretense of looking through the lockers in the cabins.

"Well?" demanded the captain of the Swallow as they came on deck again, "found any smuggled goods?"

"None," reported Silverado promptly--"none, I am pleased to say."

"Then you give us a clean sheet on health and cargo, do you?" said Broadbeam. "Reason I ask, is that we are going to swing out of harbor soon as you get through with your tomfoolery."

Just here one of the officer's assistants came up and whispered in the ear of his superior. He pointed at the forecastle.

"Yes, yes," nodded Silverado, "take a look there, and be thorough."

"Getting warm!" chuckled Dave to himself--"the precious hypocrites!"

The man went into the forecastle and came out again. He looked into the water barrel. He lifted some box covers. Just as Dave guessed he would do, he kept up all this wise pretense until he landed up against the forecastle cubby-hole.

"I have found something," he announced, after groping in the hole. He had brought forth the stone jar.

"Ah, what is this?" spoke the officer. "Captain," he added, assuming great sudden gravity as he inspected the jar, "this looks pretty serious."

"Well, what's the mare's nest now?" petulantly demanded Broadbeam.

The officer held up the jar in plain view.

"It is what we expected to find," he announced severely. "It is opium. We know that last week a tramp steamer landed a lot of the stuff on the island. The labels show that this is part of the same contraband cargo. I declare this package and the Swallow under confiscation, and arrest you. You must come to the governor."

"Oh, that so?" slowly spoke Captain Broadbeam, his shoulders hunching dangerously. "I never saw that jar before, and, shiver my timbers!" roared the incensed old captain, shaking his fist vigorously under Silverado's nose, "I don't know the stuff is opium."

"Oh, yes, captain," insisted the officer. "The labels are unmistakable. Look for yourself. Ough!"

With smart-Aleck readiness the suave Silverado untwisted the jar cover. With a sharp cry he dropped it. In a cloud, a stream, there instantly darted out from the receptacle an angry procession of hornets.

They lit on those nearest to the jar, the officer and his assistants. One of his aides was a special target. The poor fellow ran to the side to escape them. He set up renewed yells as they stuck, pestered, and stung. Then, splash! he took a reckless header into the waters of the creek to escape his pertinacious tormentors.

Silverado lost all his usual calm dignity trying to evade the little pests. He bit his lips and scowled as the captain faced him with a loud derisive guffaw.

"Here, take away your contraband goods with you," shouted Broadbeam, dropping jar and cover into the yawl, as the official hastily descended into it, a crestfallen look on his face. "Ready, there," he added to the boatswain. "Steam up."

"Aye, aye, sir."

Captain Broadbeam stepped to the little pilot house. He touched an electric button.

Dave watched the maneuver with a glowing face. He was full of the successful guess he had made concerning the planted opium, but he did not try to explain that just then.

The jar of the starting steam below communicated a vibrating thrill to his nerves. Dave ran up to Amos Fearless as the veteran diver crossed the deck.

"Good news, father!" cried Dave gayly, "We've started."

"Hey and hallo for me paternal dominions--once more for the Windjammers' Island and the stolen threasure!" shouted Pat Stoodles, cutting a caper.

"Will we find it, I wonder?" sighed the old diver thoughtfully.

"I think we shall, father," answered Dave Fearless, with confidence.

CHAPTER IX

A BOLD PROJECT

The Swallow cleared her moorings in the creek on Minotaur Island, and steamed out into the broad waters of the bay, a thing of life and beauty.

"And what's that for now?" asked Pat Stoodles of Dave, who was watching their progress and the coastline with great interest.

"I see," nodded Dave. "You mean the longboat from the governor?"

"That same, lad. Luk at 'em, now. Ever since we came into open wather they've been tearing along for the town like mad. Aha, there goes one of those measly marines overboard."

Dave ran for a telescope. He viewed the government boat with a good deal of curiosity.

The official, Silverado, stood up in the stern gesticulating with energy, and evidently inciting his men to their best efforts at the oars.

"In a hurry to reach town, it seems," muttered Pat.

"In a tremendous hurry," said Dave. "So much so, that one of the men has leaped overboard, waded ashore, and is making a lickety-switch run across lots for the town."

Dave went at once to Captain Broadbeam and apprized him of the maneuvers of their recent visitors.

"That's all right, lad," chuckled the old mariner. "Let 'em squirm. We're safe out of their clutches."

"Not so safe," spoke Dave to his father, half an hour later. "Look there."

The officer Silverado had seemingly got word to the governor of the departure of the Swallow. A few minutes after the longboat had disappeared around a neck of land, the ironclad gunboat hove into view.

She was a saucy, spiteful little craft and a fast runner. She was headed direct for the Swallow.

"Are they coming for us, captain?" inquired Amos Fearless, somewhat anxiously.

"I hope not, for their own sakes," muttered Broadbeam quickly. Then he shouted some orders down the tube and the Swallow made a spurt.

"Running away?" said Pat Stoodles. "Shure, if I was in command I'd sthand and give her one or two good welts."

"Captain Broadbeam knows his business, Mr. Stoodles," declared Dave; "you can always count on that."

Far out in the bay were a group of sandbars and several small wooded islands. The Swallow was headed for the largest of these islets. The gunboat swung a challenge signal to which the Swallow made no reply.

Then, just as the steamer, pursuant to her captain's orders, began to slow up, the ironclad fired a gun.

"Give them their walking papers, Mr. Drake," rang out Broadbeam to the boatswain.

The latter ran up a signal flag. This signified that the Swallow announced herself two-and-one-half miles from shore, and therefore out of the jurisdiction of Minotaur Island, claiming the freedom of neutral waters.

"That'll hold her for a while," gloated Stoodles. "Aha! ye'll have to take back wather now."

The gunboat reminded Dave of some spiteful being cheated out of its prey. She circled, spit steam, and went more slowly back to port.

Captain Broadbeam now ordered the Swallow just without the shoal line of a big sandy island they had neared. Here they came to anchor.

Bob Vilett came up on deck reeking with the steam and grease of the engine room.

"What's the programme, Bob?" asked Dave.

"Captain says we are going to stop here and take on ballast."

"For how long?"

"Till to-morrow, I reckon. I say, Dave, you've got your heart's desire, eh?"

"I am the happiest boy living," answered the young diver. "Something tells me we are going to get and enjoy that treasure after all mishaps and disappointments."

In order to repair the Swallow in the creek, the ballast had been taken out and the contents of the hold generally shifted about.

Now the captain set his men at work to take on new sand ballast from the island and get things in the hold in regular order.

A pulley cable was run ashore. Dave and Bob were the first to take an aerial spin along this, dangling from the big iron kettle that ran down the incline.

Dave had told Captain Broadbeam and the others of his agency in the matter of substituting the hornets for the opium. The recital had made the captain good-natured, and he had given the boys permission to rove over the sand island at will for the day.

Dave and Bob put in a pleasant hour or two talking, fishing, and discussing the probable adventures that would greet them when they again visited the Windjammers' Island.

At about five o'clock in the afternoon the work of securing ballast was completed. The captain then announced that there was some work still to do in the hold. They would make their real start with daylight.

Dave and Bob were taking a last swim in the cool of the day. A clear sky and a fine breeze made the exercise delightful. Finally they got daring one another. Dave swam to the little sand islet next to the large one. Bob beat him in a race to the third of the group.

"Come on, if you've got the nerve," hailed Dave, making a quarter-mile dash for a sand mound still beyond them.

Bob started, but turned back. Dave made port and threw himself on the dry sand to rest. He got back his breath and sat up ready to take the home course, when his eye was attracted to something on an island about a furlong beyond the one he was on.

This was the nearest of the wooded islands. Dave had not noticed it much before. What made him notice it now was that, half-hidden in a great growth of bushes and vines, he noticed a small log hut.

In front of this a mast ran up into the air. At the moment that Dave looked he saw a man fumbling at the lines along this mast. It was to raise a blue bunting.

"Hello, hello," murmured Dave slowly, staring hard and thinking desperately fast. "Why, that's easy to guess. That man is Schmitt-Schmitt."

Dave could not precisely recognize the man at such a distance, but felt sure that it was Schmitt-Schmitt. He thought this the more positively as he saw that piece of blue bunting run up the mast.

"That was one of the signals I heard Schmitt-Schmitt tell the pilot about," mused Dave. "Red for provisions, blue for sickness or help wanted. Lantern at night, bunting by day. That's it, sure. He is signaling the pilot. That island is Schmitt-Schmitt's place of hiding. Say, here's something to think about."

Dave did not stay long to think about it. His eyes brightened and he seemed moved by some inspiriting idea as he jumped into the water and was soon back in the company of his chum, Bob Vilett.

Dave was quite silent and meditative till they had reached the big sandy island. Arrived there, he slowly dressed himself.

"Come on, I'm hungry as a bear--don't want to miss a good supper, Dave," hailed Bob, starting for the Swallow.

"Hold on!" challenged Dave. "I want to tell you something before we go aboard."

"Fire away," directed Bob.

"Can you manage to get off duty about dusk?"

"There's nothing for me to do till we steam up again," replied Bob. "Why?"

"Can we get one of the small boats for an hour or two, do you think?"

Bob shook his head negatively.

"Heard the captain shut down on the chance of anybody sneaking to town and making more trouble. No, it can't be done, unless the captain gives special orders. Why?" pressed Bob curiously.

"I don't want to tell the captain what I am up to till I accomplish something," explained Dave. "I'll tell you, though, for you've got to help me."

"All right, Dave," piped Bob readily.

"We must rig up some kind of a craft to reach the first wooded island."

"What for?"

"Schmitt-Schmitt is in hiding there."

"Aha, I see!" cried Bob excitedly.

"I propose," said Dave deliberately, "that we visit him, capture him, and bring on board the Swallow--as a prisoner--the only man probably who can guide us straight to that stolen treasure."

"Famous!" cried Bob Vilett enthusiastically--"but can we do it?"

"Let's try it, anyhow," answered Dave Fearless.

CHAPTER X

THE WOODED ISLAND

Captain Broadbeam gave pretty strict orders at dusk. A watch was set with directions to allow no one to leave the Swallow. All the small boats were chained stoutly.

"We'll have to defer going ashore, or report our plans to the captain," said Bob Vilett about eight o'clock, coming up on deck with a wry face. He was in overalls and his hands covered with oil. "No go, Dave," he reported.

"You mean you can't join me?" asked Dave, in disappointment.

"That's it, Dave. There's work till twelve. I've got to stay. Say, why don't you tell the captain your idea and have him send men and a boat after Schmitt-Schmitt?"

"No," said Dave, "Captain Broadbeam wouldn't entertain the project for a moment. He is a first-class captain, but hint at anything outside of his ship, and he won't take the risk."

"What are you going to do, then?"

"Try it alone."

"Be careful, Dave. Don't undertake too much. You can never manage Schmitt-Schmitt alone. Why don't you impress Stoodles into service?"

"Mr. Stoodles is willing enough," answered Dave, "but he might bungle. It will be all I can do to get off the Swallow alone."

Dave managed this, however, a little later, without discovery. Once on the sand flat, he dragged some planks and ropes the ballast crew had left there to the other side of the island. Dave constructed quite a raft and pushed it into the water. Swimming, he propelled it before him. Within half an hour he was on the wooded island.

The first thing that caught his eye was a blue light strung from a tree at the end of the island nearer the town. Here there was a favorable natural landing-place.

"The bunting signal didn't attract attention," reasoned Dave, "so Schmitt-Schmitt has tried the lantern. Wonder if he is at the hut? I'll work my way around that direction and find out."

Dave had the bold idea in mind of capturing this man. As he went along he thought of plan after plan. If he could get Schmitt-Schmitt helpless in his power, he could convey him to the Swallow on the raft.

"The very thing," said Dave gladly, as he neared the vicinity of the hut. Lying across the top of some bushes was a fishing net. It had long rope ends. Dave with his pocket knife cut these off and thrust them in his pocket.

"Hey, what are you up to there?"

Dave thrilled at the sharp call, and turned quickly to face his challenger.

It was Schmitt-Schmitt. He had abruptly emerged from the greenery surrounding the hut. He carried a big cudgel, and as the clear moonlight revealed the face of the intruder plainly he uttered a quick gasp.

"Ha, I know you!" cried Schmitt-Schmitt, advancing with a scowling face.

"It seems so," answered Dave coolly, cautiously retreating. "You are Mr. Gerstein."

"No, you don't!" spoke the man, with a speedy leap forward.

Dave dodged, but not soon enough. The cudgel came down directly on top of his head. He saw stars, sank flat, and knew no more for fully five minutes.

Then, his lower limbs wound round and round with ropes, he struggled upon the floor of a hut.

At a table on which burned a candle sat Schmitt-Schmitt. He had just opened a bottle of lime juice and was about to pour some of its contents into a glass to refresh himself.

He suspended operations, however, as Dave struggled to an upright position, attracting his attention.

"Well," he spoke with a coarse chuckle, "how did that wallop suit you?"

Dave rubbed his sore head and made a wry grimace.

"You don't treat visitors very politely, do you?" he said.

"You're a spy, you are," spoke Gerstein sullenly, "and don't you deny it. I know you. Now then, what brought you here?"

"What brought you?" retorted Dave.

"Don't you get saucy," warned Schmitt-Schmitt. "All along you did the big things that were done in baffling the Hankers. I hear, too, you have been pretty smart with your tricks since you came to Minotaur Island."

"Of course I've been trying to do all I could to protect my rights," said Dave. "I knew you were in hiding here."

"Ha! eh?" exclaimed Schmitt-Schmitt, pricking up his ears. "How did you know that?"

"Oh, we have kept track of you," answered Dave lightly. "As soon as we found you were back of the governor and the pilot in bothering us, we naturally watched you."

Schmitt-Schmitt stared in stupefaction at Dave.

"Knew it, did you?" he muttered.

"Of course we did. We knew what you were up to. Now I can tell you, Mr. Gerstein, you will never get that treasure away from the Windjammers' Island, no matter how hard you try."

"Treasure! The Windjammers' Island!" gasped the man. "How--when--where--the--the treasure was lost at sea."

"Not a bit of it, as you and I both know," asserted Dave blithely, reading in the confusion and excitement of the man a confirmation of his suspicions. "I say the Swallow, with or without me, sails in search of that treasure at daylight. Come, sir, you have gone in with a measly crowd who will only rob you in the end. Come to Captain Broadbeam, save us the trouble of a long search, and my father will pay you all right."

Schmitt-Schmitt got up and paced the floor. He seemed thinking over what Dave had suggested. His face, however, gradually resumed its customary ferocity and cunning.

"No," he said finally, striking the table with his fist and taking in his captive's helpless situation with a good deal of satisfaction. "I have the upper hand. I keep it."

"What upper hand?" asked Dave.

"You are my prisoner. Soon the pilot will be here in response to my signal with his launch. I will take you to the island with me. I will hide you. They will not get along so grandly without you. They will delay to search for you, and delay is all I ask. Yes, yes, that is the programme."

Some whistles from craft in the bay echoed out. Schmitt-Schmitt went outside, apparently to see if some answer was coming to his signal.

"I am in it--deep," mused Dave. "Pshaw! I hate to think I shall delay and bother Captain Broadbeam."

Dave found that the ropes securing him were not very tightly arranged. They had been drawn to a loop about his waist and caught with snap and hook behind.

"If I had time I could work loose," he thought. "I have not time, so I suppose I must wait meekly and take what comes to me. Oh, by the way--that's an idea!"

The "idea" in question was suggested by a glance at the bottle and glass on the table. Dave's eyes sparkled. He fumbled under the ropes and brought out wrapped up in a fragment of paper the sample of opium he had discovered the night previous.

Frog-like he began hitching himself across the floor. Dave kept his eye anxiously fixed on the open doorway. He got to the table, reached up, dropped some grains of the drug into the glass there, and nimbly as he could hitched his way back to his former position.

Two minutes later Schmitt-Schmitt reappeared. He went at once to the table, poured out a drink, settled back in his chair, and said complacently:

"My friend will soon be here. Do your friends also know I am here?"

"Oh, dear, you mustn't expect me to tell any secrets to a fellow who won't join in with us," said Dave.

"Maybe after a little solitude you will be willing to talk," observed Schmitt-Schmitt meaningly.

"All right--we'll see," said Dave, with affected unconcern.

Dave's eyes sparkled as Schmitt-Schmitt began to blink. He was delighted as the man fell back drowsily in the chair.

"Now's my chance," said Dave, as a prolonged snore announced the complete subjugation of Schmitt-Schmitt to the influence of the drug.

Dave did some brisk moving about. He managed to get to a cupboard. He could not reach his own pocket knife. In the cupboard he found a case knife and set at work sawing away the ropes that bound him.

He laughed at his rare success, as stretching his cramped limbs he went outside for a moment.

"I don't want to delay," he thought. "That signal may bring the pilot at any moment, and that means two to handle instead of one. This is just famous. Better than I planned out. How shall I get Schmitt-Schmitt to the raft?"

Dave found an old wicker mattress on the rude porch of the hut. It had rope ends to attach as a hammock. He took the precaution to tie Schmitt-Schmitt's wrists and ankles together with ropes.

Then Dave dragged the insensible man from his chair across the floor and let him down flat on the wicker mattress.

It required all his strength to pull this drag and its burden the two hundred feet required down the beach.

"The mischief!" cried Dave, as, panting, he reached the spot where he had left the rudely improvised raft.

It was nowhere in sight, and he readily surmised that he had carelessly left it too near the surf, which had carried it away.

"Whatever am I to do now?" thought Dave. "I can't swim to the Swallow with this man. I must find the material for a new raft. Pshaw! there's a call to time."

Dave glanced keenly seawards. Then with due haste he dragged mattress and burden back into the brush out of sight.

Peering thence, he watched a little launch making for the wooded island at the point where the blue signal shone.

"The pilot, of course," said Dave. "He has come to see his friend. What will he do when he fails to find him?"

With some anxiety Dave Fearless watched the little launch come nearer and nearer to the wooded island.

CHAPTER XI

A RACE FOR LIFE

"Yes, it is the pilot," said Dave to himself, as the launch drove directly into the little natural landing-place where the blue lantern swung.

Dave peered from his bushy covert and closely watched the maneuvers of its occupant.

The pilot ran the nose of the craft well into the sand, shut off the power, and leaped ashore.

Dave saw him take up a basket and watched him depart for the hut. As soon as some trees shut him out from view Dave leaped on board of the launch.

A momentary inspection of the operating lever and steering gear told Dave that he could easily navigate the boat.

"I must lose no time," he thought. "My only chance of getting away with Schmitt-Schmitt is in taking the launch."

Dave forthwith dragged his unconscious captive to the launch. It was no easy task to get that bulky individual aboard. Dave accomplished it, however, and then paused to catch his breath and wipe the perspiration from his face.

"Hi! hi! hi!"

A ringing yell, or rather three of them, uttered in rapid and startling succession, made Dave turn with a shock.

Looking down the beach, he saw the pilot running towards him at full speed. The latter had evidently visited the hut, had found it vacated, and coming out to look for his missing friend, had discovered the launch in the hands of a stranger.

Dave made no reply. He sprang to the little lever, reversing it, and the launch slid promptly back into the water. Swinging the steering gear south, Dave turned on full power.

"Stop. I'll shoot--stop! stop!" panted the pilot, gaining on Dave with prodigious bounds of speed.

Dave kept his hand on the lever, his eyes fixed ahead. Suddenly----

Bang--ping! a shot whistled past his ear. Dave crouched and darted a quick glance backward. The pilot, coming to a standstill, was firing at him from a revolver.

Dave saw a point of refuge ahead. This was a broken irregular wooded stretch, well-nigh impassable on foot. As a second shot sounded out, Dave curved around this point of land.

He was now out of view of the pilot, who would find great difficulty in crossing the stretch lying between them, as it was marshy in spots. Dave lined the shore farther on, feeling pretty proud of the success of his single-handed enterprise.

"Why," he mused, "we have the game in our own hands completely now. I wonder what father and Captain Broadbeam will say to all this. Of course they won't fancy such a guest as Schmitt-Schmitt, but they must see how holding him a harmless captive helps our plans."

Dave made a sweep with the launch to edge the rounding end of the island. Here it narrowed to about two hundred feet. It would now be a straight bolt past the same islets to where the Swallow was.

"Won't do--the gunboat, sure as shingles!" spoke Dave suddenly.

Almost directly in his course, and bearing down upon him, was the ironclad. In that clear moonlight everything was plain as in daylight. Dave could see the people on board the gunboat, and they could see him--without doubt.

In fact, someone in uniform leaned over the bow of the ironclad in his direction. Dave caught an indistinct hail. He paid no attention to it.

He acted with the precipitancy of a school fugitive running away from a truant officer. He saw just one chance to evade an unpleasant overhauling by the ironclad, and took it.

This was to instantly steer to the north and shoot down the narrow neck of water lying between the wooded island and the nearest sand island.

Dave knew that this channel must be quite shallow. He doubted if the cumbersome iron-clad could navigate it. Even if it tried to, it would be some minutes before its crew could swing around into position to make the chase.

The launch took the channel like an arrow. Dave's spirits rose high, notwithstanding some loud and quite peremptory hails from the direction of the gunboat.

"Better than before," soliloquized Dave. "I can swing around the sandbars directly to the anchorage of the Swallow."

Glancing back, Dave saw that the gunboat did not intend to follow the course he had taken. That craft had stopped and put about.

"They must suspect that something's not exactly right," calculated Dave. "The mischief--that was close. Ouch! I'm hit."

Dave went keeling over from the bow seat. Very suddenly, from some bushes on the wooded island, there were two sharp flashes and reports. One bullet whizzed past his head, the second plowed a furrow across his forearm. It was not deep, but the wound bled, and the surprise and shock sent Dave over backwards.

The worst of it was that he jerked the lever, and this, turning the launch, sent its nose directly into shore, and there the boat stuck, vibrating with the impact of the still working machinery. The pilot instantly ran from cover towards the boat, flourishing the weapon in his hand. He had crossed the island, it seemed, to head off the launch, and it looked as though Dave was doomed to disaster in his present enterprise.

Dave scrambled to get back to the lever, and reverse the launch. As he did so his hand touched something lying upon straps at the side of the seat pit.

It was a rifle. Dave seized it, jerked it and its fastenings free, and extended it directly at the running figure ashore.

"Get back," he shouted. "Drop that pistol, Mr. Pilot, or there will be trouble."

The pilot, with a howl of rage, halted short. He flung the revolver down. Dave guessed that it was now empty.

As Dave touched the lever and got out into the channel again, he saw the pilot running back along the beach. He was headed for the end of the island in the direction of the ironclad, and yelling out some information to those aboard at the top of his bellowing voice.

"Now for a spurt," said Dave.

The channel was about a mile long. Dave came to its end in fine spirits. It was a clear run now past the two outer sand islands, and a half-mile turn would bring him to the Swallow.

He proceeded more leisurely now, for it did not seem possible that the ironclad could make the opposite circuit in time to head him off. Where the sand hills dropped, however, Dave had a view across the two next islands.

"They are after me," he exclaimed. "The pilot has advised them of the real state of affairs, and it's a sharp run. Full power--go!"

Dave had made out the gunboat whizzing down the channel between the two outer sand islands. She was forcing full speed. It was a question whether the gunboat would not emerge first into the open sea and block his course.

Dave put on power that made the little launch strain and quiver from stem to stern. He was terribly excited and anxious. His breath came in quick jerks, his heart beat fast.

"Close shave," he panted, "but I've made it."

Two hundred feet down the channel was the gunboat, as Dave crossed her outlet. The ironclad swung out after him not one minute later.

The launch fairly skimmed the water. The ironclad loomed portentously near, but Dave felt that, no mishap occurring, he would win the race.

"They've got me, I guess," he gasped a second later.

A flash, a loud boom, and a terrific concussion plunged Dave into a condition of extreme confusion and uncertainty.

The ironclad had fired a shot. It had struck the stern of the launch, splintering it clear open. A great shower of water deluged Dave and his insensible captive.

Dave regarded the damage done with grave dismay--the stern had sunk and the launch was now on a slant.

In fact, the rear portion of the boat was under water to the rail.

Only by keeping up power could the launch be prevented from filling and going down. Dave never let go his grasp on the lever. He held firmly to the last notch in the indicator.

As he turned the end of the last sand island, the maneuver made the launch wabble. Just here a second gun was fired from the ironclad. The shot went far wide of its intended mark, but a vital alarm urged Dave to change his course.

The launch went sideways, and a sudden inrush of water sunk her to the middle. Dave headed for shore. There the launch struck, a wreck.

Down the shore lay the Swallow. Active lights were bobbing about her deck, so Dave knew that the crew had been aroused by the firing at sea.

His first thought was to get Schmitt-Schmitt out of the half-submerged launch. He dragged his captive to the beach, then he took a look at the gunboat.

"Why," exclaimed Dave, in mingled astonishment and satisfaction, "she's grounded."

Apparently the ironclad had struck some treacherous sandbar over which the light swift launch had glided in safety. Loud orders, quick bells, and whistles made a small babel aboard the craft in distress.

Dave glanced down calculatingly at his helpless captive. He must get him to the Swallow. But how?

The pit crate of the launch had floated up as the craft filled with water. Dave waded to it, pulled it ashore, and rolled Schmitt-Schmitt across it.

He was now quite hidden from the view of those aboard of the gunboat, but he feared they might send a yawl on an investigating expedition.

Dave swam, pushing the crate before him. Often he glanced back. There was no pursuit. More hopefully and nearer and nearer he approached the Swallow. With a kind of a faint cheer Dave hailed her as he came within hearing distance.

"Ahoy, there!" rang back Captain Broadbeam's foghorn voice, as he gazed down at crate, burden, and swimmer.

"It's me--Dave Fearless," began the latter.

"Bet it is! Had to have a rumpus, eh? What was the shooting? Lower away there, men. Two of you, eh? What! that rascally pawnbroker, Gerstein!" fairly yelled the captain, as by stages Dave and his captive came nearer, were helped by the crew, and now gained the deck of the Swallow.

"Yes, Captain Broadbeam," nodded the nearly exhausted Dave. "The gunboat--after us--suggest you get away--at once--excuse--weak and dizzy----"

And just then Dave Fearless sank flat to the deck of the Swallow, overcome completely after the hardest work he had ever done in his life.

CHAPTER XII

OVERBOARD

"What does he say, Captain Broadbeam?" asked Dave Fearless.

"Mum as an oyster, lad."

"Won't talk, eh?" remarked Dave's father. "Nothing come of giving him free board, and after all the trouble you had, Dave, in getting him onto the Swallow."

"You forget, father," reminded Dave, "it is one enemy the less to worry about."

"The lad's right," declared Captain Broadbeam. "It means a good deal to clip the wings of the main mover in this scheme against us. If Gerstein, or Sehmitt-Schmitt as he calls himself, won't do us any good, at least he can do us no harm as long as we hold him a prisoner. I reckon those fellows back at Minotaur Island are a little dazed at the slick way we disappeared,-- ship, their crony, and all."

Bob Vilett, seated in the cabin with the others, laughed heartily.

"It was a big move and a good one, that of yours in capturing this rascal," he declared to Dave. "Now we certainly have the field to ourselves. The governor and the pilot can't follow us, for they don't know where we have gone. No one is on this treasure search except ourselves. It's a clear field, as I say."

"Until we reach the Windjammers' Island," suggested Dave. "I wouldn't wonder if Gerstein had left Captain Nesik and the others there, probably guarding the treasure while awaiting his return."

The Swallow had got away from the vicinity of Minotaur Island two days previous. Just as soon as, after his exciting capture of Gerstein, Dave had sufficiently recovered to explain matters to Captain Broadbeam, the latter had ordered on full steam, leaving the ironclad stuck on the sandbar.

Gerstein raved like a madman when the drug Dave had given him began to lose its effect. He threatened all kinds of things--the law, for one, for kidnapping--but Captain Broadbeam only laughed at him.

"Just one word, my hearty," he observed spicily. "As long as you behave yourself, outside of every man aboard having his eye on you to look out for tricks, you'll have bed and food with the best of us. Try any didos, though, and I clap you into irons--understand?"

Gerstein became at once sullen and silent. When he came on deck after that he spoke to nobody. Most of the time he remained shut up by himself in the little cabin apportioned to him.

The second day out Captain Broadbeam sought an interview with him. It was after a talk with Amos Fearless.

He offered Gerstein a liberal share of the treasure if he would divulge its whereabouts and tell what had become of the Raven and her crew.

Gerstein declined to say a word. He simply regarded the captain in a mocking, insolent way. It was evident that the fellow appreciated the full value of his knowledge concerning the treasure.

"He's counting on getting away from us somehow, before the cruise is over," reported Captain Broadbeam to his friends, "or he is taking chances on our running into a nest of his friends when we reach the Windjammers' Island."

The Swallow had a delightful run to Mercury Island. Before they reached it Gerstein was placed in the hold, and there closely guarded by two mariners until they had provisioned up and were once more on their way.

Dave had little to do except to wait the end of their cruise, yet he put in some busy hours. For three days he kept Stoodles at his side at the table in the captain's cabin, questioning him on every detail about the lay and outlines of the island they were sailing to. Then he made a chart of the island, and as near as possible from memory marked in the other island where they had recovered possession of the Swallow after it had been stranded during a cyclone.

The weather changed suddenly a day or two out from Mercury Island. They rode into a fierce northeaster, and it rained nearly all the time, with leaden skies and a choppy sea.

Dave was a good deal below. One afternoon, returning from a brief visit to Bob Vilett, as he was making for the cabin passageway, a chink of light attracted his attention.

It emanated from a crack in the paneling of the cabin occupied by Gerstein. Dave drew nearer to the chink, and could look quite clearly into the compartment that housed the person in whom he was naturally very much interested at all times.

"H'm!" said Dave, with a bright flicker in his eye. "He's making a chart, too, is he?"

The daylight was so dim that Gerstein had a lighted candle on the table at which he sat. Spread out before him was a sheet of heavy manila paper. It bore black outlines as if an irregular body of land, and had crosses and dots all over it.

At this Gerstein was working, thoughtfully scanning it at times and then making additions to it. Dave believed that it had something to do with the treasure.

"Our treasure," he reflected, "and I'll play something else than the spy if I get a chance to look over that chart, whatever it is."

He watched the man's movements for over half an hour. Then Gerstein folded up the paper, placing it in a thin tin tobacco box. This he secured in a pocket in the blue shirt he wore, buttoning the pocket flap securely.

Dave got no further sight of the mysterious paper, if such it was, during the next week. He felt himself justified in trying to get a chance to secure the little tin box. Twice he visited Gerstein's cabin secretly, while its occupant was on deck. Gerstein, however, apparently carried the box with him wherever he went.

One night, when he slept, Dave crept into the cabin, the door of which for a wonder had been left unlocked. He ransacked Gerstein's clothing, but with no result.

"Got it somewhere in bed with him," thought Dave. "I don't dare to try and find it, though. I would surely wake him up. I believe I will tell Captain Broadbeam about the little tin box. If it in any way concerns this treasure, why haven't we the right to take it away from Gerstein, even by force?"

Before Dave had an opportunity to consult with Captain Broadbeam, however, something transpired that changed all his plans.

It was a dark and stormy night. The weather had been rough all day. Dave came on deck about eight o'clock to find the captain on duty. A few men were making things tidy about the stern deck.

The Swallow was plowing the water, slanted like a swordfish in action. Dave held to a handle at the side of the cabin, peering into the darkness that hung about them like a pall.

According to the calculations of the captain they were somewhere in the vicinity of the Windjammers' Island--probably within fifty miles of it, he had told Amos Fearless at sunset.

As Dave stood there, braced and exhilarated by the dash of wind and spray, he saw Gerstein suddenly rush up the cabin stairs.

"Hello, what's up with him, I wonder," thought Dave.

The remark was caused by a view of the face of the fellow as he passed a lantern set near the forecastle. Gerstein seemed frightfully agitated. Heedless of the slippery deck, he plunged along towards the stern. Once or twice a lurch threatened to bring him clear over the rail and into the sea.

Dave could not resist following him to learn the cause of his perturbation. A swing of the boat sent him clinging to the rail. Holding firmly, Dave, within twelve feet of the stern, saw Gerstein dash in among the men busy there and heard him shout out:

"Barlow--quick. Is he here?"

"Here I am," answered the owner of that name, looking around from his task of lashing down the cover of a water butt.

"My shirt--your shirt--the one you loaned me while I had mine washed," spoke Gerstein, in an anxious, gasping tone. "I gave it back to you this afternoon."

"Yes, you did," nodded Barlow.

"Where is it? Have you it on--say, quick!"

"Threw it under my bunk. In the forecastle. Bunk nearest the gangway. Hey, you've no sea legs, that's sure."

A lurch of the steamer had sent Gerstein off his footing. He went headlong. His head struck the side, and for a second he lay stunned.

Before he had fairly got to his feet, Dave Fearless had acted under the impulse of a very vivid suggestion.

From what he had seen and heard he felt certain that Gerstein wanted the shirt he had borrowed because he had left something in his pocket.

"That tin box, I'll bet--why not?" cried Dave, making a dash in the direction of the forecastle.

Dave was so full of his idea that he did not take the trouble to look back to see if Gerstein was coming, too. He got to the forecastle, was down the gangway fast as he could go, and a second later was groping under Barlow's bunk.

"Here it is," he said, pulling out the garment in question. "Something in the pocket, too, yes, it's the box--the little tin box, I can tell by the feeling. Good!"

Dave hurried back up the steps. He just cleared them as Gerstein plunged rather than ran towards them. A steady light shone here.

"Say," bolted out Gerstein, at once recognizing the garment in Dave's hand, "that's my shirt."

"No, it isn't," declared Dave, swinging back as Gerstein made a grab at the garment. "It belongs to Barlow."

"I have something in it."

"I know you have."

"Ha, you spy! Let go, let go."

The result of a general mixing up of Dave and Gerstein was that each now had hold of the coveted garment.

As Gerstein spoke last he sagged and swung Dave around to one side.

Dave held on tightly. Suddenly Gerstein made a feint. He slackened the tension by a bend forward, one hand swung out.

Dave received a heavy blow at the side of the head. It was totally unexpected, and he loosed his grip and went reeling backward.

At that moment a terrific wave swept over the deck. Dave was submerged and carried along.

He tried in vain to catch at something. The tilt of the steamer sent him shooting outward, and the next moment he plunged over the rail into the sea below.

CHAPTER XIII

ADRIFT ON THE PACIFIC

The sea had been the natural element of Dave Fearless since his earliest childhood. In the stress of his present predicament, however, he felt that he was in the most critical situation of his life.

A great wave received him as he went overboard. A second swept over it, ingulfing him for a full half-minute, and he was battling desperately with the vortex caused in part by the storm, in part by the swiftly-moving steamer.

As the youth emerged into less furious elements, his first thought was of the Swallow. He dashed the water from his eyes with one hand and strained his sight.

"It's no use," he spoke. "She'll be out of reach in two minutes."

Dave did not try to shout. It would have done him no good, he realized. As he was lifted up on the crest of wave after wave, the vague spark of light that designated the Swallow grew fainter and farther away. Finally it was shut out from view altogether.

The water was buoyant, and aided by his expertness as a swimmer Dave did not sink at all, and found little difficulty in keeping afloat. But how long could this state of things last? he asked himself.

There was not the least possible hope of any aid from the Swallow. He had gone overboard unseen by any person except Gerstein.

"He will tell no one," reflected Dave. "In the first place it would be dangerous for him to do so, for they would suspect treachery on his part. In the next place he is probably glad to get rid of me. Unless Bob or father look into my stateroom, I shall not be missed before morning. By that time----"

Dave halted all conjecture there. The present was too vital to waste in idle surmises. He planned to use all the skill and endurance he possessed to keep afloat. He might do this for some hours, he calculated, unless the waves grew much rougher.

"It's a hard-looking prospect," Dave told himself, as he began to feel severely the strain of his situation. "Adrift on the Pacific! How far from land? As I know, the Swallow's course was out of the regular ocean track. The chances of ever seeing father and the others again are very slim."

Something slightly grazed Dave's arm as he concluded this rather mournful soliloquy. He grabbed out at the touch of the foreign object, but missed it. Then a second like object floated against his chest. This the lad seized.

It proved to be a piece of wood, part of a dead tree, about three inches in diameter and two feet long. Dave retained the fragment, although scarcely with the idea of using it as a float.

To his surprise these fragments, some large, some small, continued to pass him. In fact, he seemed in a sort of wave-channel, which caught and confined them, forming a species of tidal trough.

One piece was of quite formidable size. Dave threw his arms over it with a good deal of satisfaction, for it sustained his weight perfectly.

"Queer how I happened right into their midst. Where do they come from, anyhow?" reflected Dave. "Is it a hopeful sign of land?"

There was a lull in the tempest finally, but the darkness still hung over all the sea like a pall. Dave longed for daybreak. The discovery of the driftwood had given him a good deal of courage and hope.

For over eight hours Dave rocked and drifted, at the mere caprice of the waves. Wearied, faint, and thirsty, he tried to cheer himself thinking of the possibility of land near at hand.

Daylight broke at last, but a dense haze like a fog hung over the waters for an hour before the sun cleared it away. Eagerly Dave scanned in turn each point of the compass. A great sigh of disappointment escaped his lips.

"No land in sight," he said; "just the blank, unbroken ocean."

His plight was a dispiriting one. Dave felt that unless succor came in some shape or other, and that, too, very soon, his chances of ever seeing home and friends again were indeed remote.

He noted the widespread mass of driftwood with friendly eyes, for it broke the monotony of the green expanse that tired the sight with its illimitable continuity.

"There's a pretty big piece of driftwood," Dave said, looking quite a distance towards a larger object than he had yet seen. It rose and fell with the swaying of the wave. "If I could find a few such pieces I might construct a raft."

Dave began to swim off in the direction of the object in the distance. A great cry of joy escaped his lips as he neared it.

"It is not a log," he shouted rapturously, "but a boat. A small yawl. Oh, dear, but I am thankful!"

In his urgency to reach the boat Dave let go of the piece of driftwood that had served him so well. His eyes grew bright and he forgot all his discomfort and suffering.

With a kind of cheer Dave lifted himself over the side of the little yawl. It was flimsy, dirty, and old. The prow was splintered, one of the seats was broken out, but Dave sank down into the craft with a luxurious sense of relief and delight.

There were no oars, but Dave did not think much of that. He had something under him to sustain him. That was the main thing for the present.

"I can make rude oars of some of the driftwood and the front seat," he calculated. "If it rains I shall have water, and there are clouds coming up fast in the west now. I may catch some fish. What's in there, I wonder," and Dave pulled open the door of the little locker.

"Hurrah!" he shouted this time, utterly unable to control his intense satisfaction. Lying in the locker was a rudely made reed basket. In this were two bottles. Dave speedily assured himself that they held water, warm and brackish, but far from unwelcome to the taste.

About twenty hardtack cakes and a chunk of cheese completed the contents of the basket.

"I never ate such a meal before," jubilated Dave, having satisfied his hunger and carefully repacked the supplies. He paused to read a part of a label pasted across the front of one of the bottles of water. "This came from the Raven."

Dave had a right to think this. At one time the bottle had held some kind of table sauce. Written under the label were the words "Captain's table, Raven."

"The boat, too, must have belonged to the Raven" said Dave, "although I don't know that surely. It looks as if some one of Captain Nesik's crew had put to sea in this yawl, and was probably lost in the storms of the last week."

A great rain came up about an hour later. There was not much wind. Following the rain a dense mist shut out sea and sky.

Dave could only drift at the will of the waves. He had it in mind to construct some kind of oars, but he did not know the distance or even the direction of land.

The day grew well on into the afternoon. Dave had removed the door of the locker. He had also gathered into the boat the longest pieces of driftwood he could find. Fortunately he had discovered in the locker several pieces of fine tarred rope, which would prove a great help in making the oars. He was laying out his work when a curious flapping noise made him look up. He sprang to his feet. Pouncing down upon him were four immense birds. They were not eagles, but fully twice as large as any eagle he had ever seen.

They attacked Dave in unison. One clawed into his left arm while another gave him a severe blow with one of its wings, swooped down upon the exposed reed basket, seized it, and flew away with it. Dave snatched up a piece of driftwood.

He shouted to frighten the birds, swinging his weapon among them vigorously. One he disabled and it fell into the water and floated out of sight, the other two he finally beat off.

The loss of the provision basket troubled Dave severely. He sank breathless into the boat, his face and hands badly scratched and bleeding.

The next instant, to the infinite surprise of Dave Fearless, a gruff voice sounded through the mist:

"Ahoy there! What's the rumpus?"

CHAPTER XIV

STRANGE COMPANIONS

Dave knew at once that his shouts at the large birds must have attracted the attention of the person who was now hailing him.

"Ahoy, yourself!" he cried, starting to his feet and peering expectantly through the mist in the direction from which the challenge had come.

In a few moments the outline of a yawl somewhat larger than the one Dave was in loomed up in the near distance. A man was seated in its bow, while two others rowed the boat.

They came alongside. All three looked haggard and worn out. In the bottom of their boat lay a broken demijohn. They reminded Dave of sailors he had often seen on shipboard getting over a debauch.

"Why," said the man in the bow, staring in amazement at Dave, "if it isn't young Fearless, the diver!"

"I remember you, Mr. Daley," responded Dave, recognizing the speaker as one of the crew of the Raven. Dave had a dim memory, too, of having seen Daley's two companions with Captain Nesik's crew.

Daley drew the two yawls close together with a boathook, and he and Dave were face to face.

"Young Fearless of the Swallow," he kept saying, in a marveling tone. "And in this fix. Why, where did you ever come from?"

"Where did you, Mr. Daley?" inquired Dave directly. "Mine is a pretty long story--suppose you tell yours first?"

"Huh, that won't take much time," muttered Daley, with a savage kick at the fragments of the demijohn. "We stole all that gold from you. Little good did it do us. Captain Nesik and the Hankers, after they marooned you fellows, made a landing and divided up the gold into boxes. They put them on the Swallow. Well, when the Swallow parted from the Raven in a cyclone, she went down--gold, men aboard, and all."

"And the Raven?" inquired Dave.

"She drove on the rocks and has been disabled ever since. It would take a big steamer to pull her into service again," explained Daley. "After she got into that fix Nesik decided to desert her. They made a camp on land on the west island of those you know about."

"What about the natives?" inquired Dave.

"They seemed to have all gone back to the main island except a few. These hung around and spied on us; most of them Nesik shot. He landed lots of provender and rum from the Raven. For a week Nesik let the men have their fill. He and the Hankers and that pawnbroker fellow----"

"Gerstein?" suggested Dave.

"Yes, Gerstein," nodded Daley. "Well, those four took the longboat which was saved from the wreck and went scouting, they called it. They went away and returned for several days. One day they came back on foot without the longboat, and said that it and Gerstein had gone down in a quicksand. The men began to grow restive after another week. They couldn't understand what Nesik was lying idle for. They wondered what made him and Cal Vixen the diver and the Hankers so contented to just squat down and loaf. The men got cross when Nesik cut down grub rations. A deputation waited on him."

"What was the result?" inquired Dave, with great interest.

"Nesik told them to do what they liked and go where they liked. Said he was going to take his chances, waiting for a ship to come along. Result was, one by one the small craft of the Raven were stolen. We nabbed this boat one night and put to sea. We were bound to make some kind of a try to get away from those islands."

"Have you any idea where we are now?" inquired Dave.

"Sure, I have," answered Daley. "We're in one of those tidal channels that run around the Windjammers' Island so freely. That's a queer thing about these diggings. A fellow can row miles and drift back to the islands. Those channels are regular whirlpools in a storm."

"And what are you thinking of doing now?" asked Dave.

"Getting back to land of course. We wouldn't run across a ship in a hundred years on this out-of-the-way route. We can never hope to row thousands of miles to a continent coast. No--provender being gone, and especially the rum, we don't feel quite as bold as we did when we started out," confessed Daley, with a dejected air.

"No," put in one of his companions lazily, "we'll go back and take pot-luck with what's left of the Raven crowd."

"If they'll have us," put in his companion. "Looked to me all along as if for some purpose or other Nesik wanted to get rid of us."

"You're right there, mate," declared Daley. "I've thought that, too, many a time. Maybe he and his cronies calculated there would be more grub around with fewer mouths to feed."

Dave thought over all the men had said. He fancied that he guessed out the reason why Nesik was so willing to have his men leave him. He knew that he would be asked to give information in return for what he had received. Dave tried to decide how far he dared to trust the three castaways.

"Now then," just as he expected, Daley spoke, "we've told you our story. How about yours? That's a Raven boat there you're in. How did you get it?"

"I found it drifting loose a few hours ago," said Dave.

"That's likely enough," said Daley suspiciously, "but where was you waiting for such things to drift around loose?"

"I was floating on a piece of driftwood," explained Dave. "You know you people marooned us on the island."

"I didn't," declared Daley; "that was Nesik's work."

"You helped," said Dave, "and you've had nothing but bad luck since. Now, Mr. Daley, I'm going to tell you something. You think the Swallow was lost in the cyclone."

"Know it. Men, gold, and all."

"No," said Dave, watching his man closely to note the effect of his disclosures. "The Swallow was not lost at all."

Daley stared hard and incredulously at Dave.

"How do you know?" he asked.

"Because I was aboard of her not twenty-four hours since. The truth is, in that cyclone she was driven ashore on the west island you speak about. There Captain Broadbeam and the rest of us discovered her. We found Mr. Drake, the boatswain; Bob Adams, the engineer, and Mike Conners, the cook, prisoners on board."

"That's right," nodded Daley; "those fellows wouldn't come in with us, and Nesik put them in irons. Go on."

"We also found some labeled boxes in the hold."

"The treasure!" cried Daley excitedly. "Alas, yes, it was all divided and made into portions, so much for the Hankers, so much for Nesik, so much for the crew. Why, we saw the Hankers divide it with our own eyes, didn't we, mates?"

"That we did," declared his two companions in unison.

"So Mr. Drake told us," resumed Dave. "Well, we liberated our friends, got the Swallow in trim, and steamed away from the Windjammers' Island about three weeks ago."

"With all that gold!" cried Daley, with disappointed but covetous eyes. "Oh, my mates, think of it!"

"No," interrupted Dave, "we thought the gold was there. The second home port we reached we opened the boxes to see."

"It must have been a sight," said Daley gloatingly.

"It was," nodded Dave, with a queer little smile--"sand, lead, old junk, every box full of them, and not a gold coin there."

Daley sprang up in the boat with a wild cry. His companions partook of his excitement.

"Then--then----" panted Daley, with blazing eyes.

"Why, the Nesik crowd just deluded you poor foolish fellows. Exactly as he did us," spoke Dave quietly, but with a definite emphasis. "As I say, there was none of the treasure in the boxes. Where was it, then? Easy to guess. It was put in the boxes to delude you fellows and later secretly removed to the Raven. Nesik intended to lose the Swallow some way. The cyclone helped him out."

Daley drew out a long-bladed knife. He began abusing Nesik and the Hankers. He slashed the air in a frantic manner.

"I'll kill them for this, I'll kill them!" he raved. "Men, you'll help me? Why," he exclaimed suddenly, "then the gold must be on the Raven, stuck on the rock, eh?"

"Hardly," answered Dave. "No, Nesik intended losing the Swallow, sailing for South America, getting rid of you fellows cheap, and then he and the Hankers and Gerstein would make a grand division of the spoils. Their plans miscarried. The Raven got wrecked. Don't you see they got you all ashore quick as they could? Without doubt those mysterious days of scouting in the longboat, as you call it, were devoted to getting the gold ashore to some safe and secret hiding-place."

"Then we'll have our share," shouted Daley. "Mates, for shore; for shore, mates, to find those measly robbers, to pounce on them and make them give up what belongs to us. Ha, more," declared Daley. "We'll kill them off; well take it all."

"Why, Mr. Daley," quietly suggested Dave, "it appears to me you are forgetting something."

"What's that?"

"That treasure belongs to my father and myself."

Daley looked sheepish, then surly.

"If you should get hold of it what could you do with it?" pursued Dave. "You can't spend it on the Windjammers' Island. You can never get it away from there except in a stanch vessel, such as may not come along for years. I should think," added Dave, "after all the trouble you have seen grow out of the Hankers stealing what was not their own, you would take a new tack."

"How, a new tack?" demanded Daley, surlily surveying Dave from under his bushy, bent brows.

"Be square and honest. The Raven people have deceived you. I have a proposition to make you. Put this whole matter in my hands, promise to help me work it out as I think best, and I'll guarantee you two things."

"What are they?" demanded Daley.

"First, that I will soon locate the hiding-place of the treasure--which you never may."

"That's so," mumbled one of Daley's companions, "everything has been queered that we tried to do so far."

"Secondly," added Dave, "when that treasure is found, I promise, if you come in with me, to give each of you a liberal share of it."

CHAPTER XV

A PERILOUS CRUISE

The sailor Daley sat down quietly in the bow of the yawl, his face beaming.

"Do you mean that, Fearless?" he said.

"I certainly do," answered Dave.

"You want us to side with you?"

"I have said so, Mr. Daley, haven't I?" asked Dave pleasantly.

"Make it a bargain, Daley," advised one of his companions eagerly. "He's a smart lad, and his talk is square, although we have treated him low and shabby."

"Never mind that," said Dave lightly. "You were in bad company, that's all. Make it business, up and down. My father and I came here to get a fortune which we had rightfully inherited. The Hankers have tried to steal it. We shall get that fortune yet. Isn't it better for you people to be in on the winning side?"

"Fearless," said Daley, "there's my hand. It's a compact, is it?"

"True and faithful," answered Dave, and they shook hands all around. "Now let me tell you that the Swallow is in fine trim, is cruising around these waters somewhere. She is bound, of course, to land on the Windjammers' Island. Get these boats there if you know how to do it, and we'll soon get into some kind of action that is bound to bring us up against Captain Broadbeam and the others, who will be true friends to you if you'll only do the right thing."

Dave felt that he had gained a decided victory in making these men his allies. Without their help he could not reach land. They could guide him to the land camp of Captain Nesik. The four of them could resist attacks of the natives if they ran across them, where one might fail.

Dave reasoned that if the men changed their minds later and attempted any treachery, it would be at a time when he and his friends were prepared to meet and thwart it.

Dave had confidence in the belief that in some way he would find the Swallow or the Swallow would find him.

His previous stirring adventures, among the Windjammers and with the Raven crowd, had brought hardship and endurance that made him now hopeful and courageous and quick to see a way to meet a situation and conquer it.

In fact, Dave's career had made considerable of a man of him. It had taught him self-reliance, and he was pleased to notice how readily the three castaways recognized him as a leader.

They acted like new men under the spur of new hopes. They evidently believed in Dave. It was some time, however, before Daley would consent to forego his thirstings for revenge against Nesik and the Hankers.

"Don't you go for to spoil everything by thinking up a rumpus," advised one of the sailor's companions. "Young Fearless means what he says. Let's rest on that, say I, and follow his orders."

"I have none to give at present," said Dave. "When I do, I am sure we will work in harmony all right. Mr. Daley, you are the pilot. Can we reach the Windjammers' Island in any way?"

"I know the point of the compass all right," asserted Daley. "The course may be a little blind until this mist rises, but--to your oars, men, and strike due west. That way," and Daley indicated the direction. "Get aboard, Fearless. It's most comfortable in the stern."

"Shall we tow the smaller boat?" inquired the young diver.

"What's the use? We don't need it, and it would only hamper us. There you are, neat and tidy."

They cast the smaller boat adrift. Dave settled down comfortably in the stern of the larger yawl.

"My!" he soliloquized, "when I think of my forlorn chances when I went overboard from the Swallow last night and this comfort and security, I'm a very thankful boy."

Dave had not had a wink of sleep for over thirty-six hours. He began to doze. Daley, noticing this, ceased his chatter with his companions. Dave was soon fast asleep.

He roused up with a vivid start some hours later. He had slept so profoundly, owing to a natural weariness and exhaustion after his arduous experiences, that he had not even been disturbed by a howling tempest that had come up.

The mist had dispersed, and it was night. A furious gale was blowing, and the frail yawl was riding on high waves.

Daley had crawled along the boat. He was shaking Dave vigorously by the arm. At the same time, bringing his lips close to Dave's ear, he shouted loudly a word that aroused Dave like an electric shock:

"Land!"

"What--where?" cried Dave, starting up.

"Steady, mate," warned Daley, holding Dave back in the seat. "Get your peepers wide open and all your senses woke up. Drop the oars," he yelled to his companions, "they're only in the way. Let her swing. It's drift or drown now, sure."

Dave sat for a moment grasping the sides of the yawl, and realizing that they were being driven along at a fearful rate of speed. Daley and his companions, too, were holding on for life.

"You said land," Dave shouted, trying to raise his voice above the roar of the tempest.

"Yes," answered Daley. "Now then, when we top a wave, look sharp--there!"

Daley pointed, and Dave fixed his glance steadily in the direction indicated.

"I see nothing," he said as they went up, down, and up again. "What did you mean?"

"A light--there it is."

"I see it," cried Dave.

"It must be a fire alongshore somewhere, probably the Windjammers' Island," declared Daley.

Dave continued to look. He studied the light each time he was afforded an opportunity. This was only when they climbed some mighty wave, and only for a few seconds.

"You are wrong, Mr. Daley," said Dave finally.

"Wrong about what? It's a light, I tell you."

"Yes, but not a shore light."

"You don't know that."

"Yes, I do. It moves as we move, only more steadily. It is some vessel," declared Dave. "I wouldn't wonder if it was the Swallow."

The mere conjecture excited Daley greatly. The men worked at the oars again. This, however, proved lost energy. When it resulted in one of the oars being torn from the grasp of its holder, and cast adrift into the sea, Daley uttered a heart-rending groan.

One of his mates, however, suggested something--this was to use his coat as a kind of sail. He and the other oarsman attempted this.

"We're going in the direction of the light, sure," cried Daley jubilantly.

"We're going down!" shouted the man who had suggested the impromptu sail.

Dave saw that all was over. Whether the use of the sail hastened the situation, or the little craft would have been overturned anyway by the gigantic wind that suddenly struck it, he had no time to conjecture.

In an instant the yawl was raised by a mighty force. It flopped over flat, spilling out all hands.

Dave saw his companions hurled from his sight like disappearing phantoms. His hand was held by the wrist in a rope loop he had clung to for protection since waking up.

Dave went over with the boat, under with it, and was unable to disentangle his wrist. His arm seemed broken. He was whipped about in a frightful manner.

Twice his head struck the keel of the scudding yawl, twice he was submerged, choked and blinded.

A third contact with the yawl landed a hard blow right across the temple, and Dave Fearless lost consciousness.

CHAPTER XVI

LANDED

Dave must have gone through a fearful experience during the next hour. Its details he never knew. Familiar with the chances and accidents of the seafaring situation from childhood, however, when he opened his eyes again he could figure out how kind his natural element had been to him.

He lay on a sandy shore. When his senses first came back a positive thrill permeated his frame.

A joyful cry arose to his lips. It was irrepressible. He was bruised, battered, soaked through, but the realization that he had landed, that he once more rested on firm hard soil, overcame every sensation of discomfort and pain.

"Landed," murmured Dave, in great delight, and that was the only idea he could take into his confused mind for the moment.

He opened his eyes. It was clear starlight. He lay on a sandy beach. The waves lapped him to the knees. Beside him was the yawl, stove in at one side. He was still attached to it by the wrist held firmly in the rope loop.

The yawl had proved a loyal convoy. As the tempest swept it along, Dave must have been held at least a part of the time out of the water. This had saved his life. Perhaps, he thought, he might at times also have lain across the upturned keel of the yawl.

At all events he was saved. There was not a bone in his body that did not ache. His wrist was swollen greatly and the arm was numb to the shoulder.

"I'm badly battered," reflected Dave. "I must get my arm loose some way."

The youth groped in his pocket with his free hand. It was a laborious task getting into the soaked garment. When he got his pocket knife out, Dave had to open it with his teeth.

He managed to cut the rope that imprisoned him, and fell away from the yawl with a feeling of great relief. Then he lay on the ground flat on his back, and for some moments tried to think of nothing but absolute rest and comfort.

Dave struggled to an upright position finally. He was amazed at his weakness and helplessness. Twice his feet refused to hold him up, and he fell down. His injured arm was perfectly numb and flabby at his side.

"This won't do at all," he thought, arousing himself. "I'm awful thirsty, too. Well, I may be able to crawl."

Dave attempted to go up the beach. About a hundred feet away, through breaks in a belt of green trees, he could catch the sparkle of water running over the rocks.

The moon had come up during all these various efforts to get into action. Dave could see his way clearly. He made in the direction of the water.

After slowly and painfully progressing for perhaps a hundred feet Dave found that his blood had begun to circulate. He pulled himself to his feet by means of some high bushes he had reached by this time.

Each moment his control increased over the numbed joints and muscles.

"This is better," said he, with satisfaction, as after some stumbling steps, with the aid of a dead tree branch, he was able to limp upright though slowly.

Dave reached the water, a mere rill gushing down the shore bluff over some rocks. It was clear and sparkling, and he took a deep draught of the life-giving element that invigorated him greatly.

"Hungry," thought Dave next. "Thanks to Stoodles--good!"

Right at his side Dave discovered a bush full of pods. When on the Windjammers' Island with Stoodles, the latter had shown him this very bush. Upon it grew pods full of kernels that tasted like cocoa. Dave ate plentifully, though it was not a very satisfying meal.

"Now then," he spoke. "Oh, how could I have forgotten them!" he cried with sudden self-reproachfulness.

It was quite natural in his forlorn, confused condition that Dave should first of all have thought only of himself. Still, his deep anxiety, poignantly aroused now as he thought of Daley and the others who had been in the yawl with him, showed his heart to be in the right place.

He hurried down to the beach again, in his solicitude for his late companions forgetting how crippled he was, and had several falls.

"It's no use," said Dave sadly, after over an hour's search along the lonely shore. "They must have perished, Daley and the others."

The conviction saddened the youth for a long time. He sat down thinking over things for nearly an hour.

"I don't know where I am," he said, rising to his feet, "and I must trust to luck as to what is best next to do. This must be the Windjammers' Island. I think I could tell if I could get to some high point overlooking it or a part of it."

Dave looked doubtfully up beyond the shore cliffs where the higher hills showed. It looked to be a pretty hard task to scale those heights in his present battered-up condition.

"I'm going to try it, anyhow," decided Dave, and he did.

"I can't go any farther--at least not just now," said Dave, an hour later.

He sank down on a moss-covered rock overlooking a kind of valley. Its other side, however, was higher up than the point where he was.

"I think another hundred feet will bring me to where I can get a good view," thought the young diver; "that is in daylight, and daylight will soon be here."

The pods, which tasted like cocoa, had been filling to Dave, but not exactly satisfying.

"It's like a fellow eating candy when he needs beefsteak," he mused. "I shall have to hunt up something more substantial later on."

From his previous acquaintance with the island Dave knew that there were many kinds of shellfish to be found, besides berries and other fruits, for the searching. He was not one bit afraid that he would have to starve.

"I must watch out for the natives, too," he continued. "I must devise some kind of a weapon of defense."

Dave thought over these things, lying restfully on the rock. He had about decided to resume his journey, calculating how long it would take him to reach a certain point on which his eyes were fixed.

"Hello!" he exclaimed suddenly, sitting bolt-upright.

What had attracted Dave's attention was a light. It had appeared suddenly on a ledge, almost at the top of the hill he was bent on climbing.

It was no fixed light, but a broad swaying jet of fire. Whoever held it was evidently swinging a lighted wisp of straw or something of that sort.

"I wonder what that means," mused Dave. "I wonder who it can be. Probably a native. But, native or otherwise, there is method in the way that light is moving. Yes, it certainly is a signal."

Such Dave decided it surely to be after watching the light for some minutes.

It described circular and other figures. It seemed directed at a point somewhere down the valley.

"I would like to know what is going on up there," said Dave, rousing up. "It would give me an inkling as to whom I have to deal with and where I really am."

After a further rest of a few minutes the young diver resumed the ascent of the hill.

CHAPTER XVII

A REMARKABLE SCENE

"Well, this is queer."

Dave Fearless looked curious and acted as if startled. By the time he had got near to the ledge where he had seen the mysterious signal, daylight had come.

Long since that illumination had been discontinued. Dave had paused with due caution as he approached its cause. He had lurked behind a big rock fronting the shelf of stone.

No other sound or presence was indicated, and after a spell of watchfulness Dave decided to approach closer. It was as he peered around the edge of a cavelike opening fronting the ravine that he uttered the words:

"Well, this is queer."

The cave extended back into the hill a long way. Dave could decide this by the shadows cast by a light that burned about fifteen feet from its opening. A rude earthen pot of native construction was filled with some kind of oil. A wick, made out of some fibrous plant, burned within it.

This light illuminated a long broad piece of matting laid across the floor of the cave. As Dave examined the various articles spread out on this mat, he was filled with amazement.

There were all kinds of dishes, such as Dave had seen in the homes of the Windjammers. These were made of thin bark and decorated with figures of flowers and birds outlined in berry stains.

"The wonder of it all, though," said Dave; "food, and such food--all kinds."

In the dishes were berries and other fruits, a kind of tapioca bread also. Then there were meats, all cooked and cold, and some fish the same. There were also two quite tastefully made bowls filled with a clear white liquid that Dave took to be cocoanut milk.

Dave watched for a long time. The display tempted his appetite prodigiously.

"Of course there's a proprietor for all this elegant layout," said Dave. "What's the occasion of it? Where is he?"

Dave sent a piece of stone rattling noisily into the cave, then a second. He waited and listened.

"I don't believe there is anyone in there," he decided. "I can't resist it. I don't know who this feast is spread for, but I want a share of it."

Dave stepped forward boldly now. His audacity was increased as he made out a spear standing against a rock. Dave took the precaution to arm himself with this. Then he came still nearer to the food.

Whoever had prepared the feast was, in Dave's estimation, a most admirable cook. The various articles he sampled tasted most appetizing.

"Fine as home cooking," said Dave, with satisfaction, stepping back from the mat. "One man wouldn't have all that stuff for breakfast, though. Is it some native ceremonial like Stoodles has told me about? Or does the man expect friends? That's it," Dave reasoned it out. "Maybe he has gone to meet them. I had better make myself scarce."

Dave was now satisfied that he was really on the Windjammers' Island. The articles in the cave were in a measure familiar to him. Then, too, a glance from the cliffs as he had ascended them had shown a distant coastline, suggesting precisely the spot where Captain Broadbeam, himself, and the others had been marooned.

Dave resolved to appropriate the weapon he had taken up. He started to leave the cave and retrace his steps to the beach. At the entrance he paused abruptly and started back.

"Too late," he exclaimed; "someone is coming."

Dave had almost run out upon two men. A curious circumstance prevented them seeing him. They were approaching from the direction opposite to that from which he himself had come in reaching the cave.

Both were natives. The minute Dave saw them he instantly recognized them as belonging to the Windjammers' tribe of which his friend Pat Stoodles had once been king.

One of them was a thin, mean-looking fellow, scrawny and wild-eyed. He was creeping on hands and knees along the path. His pose and manner suggested the utmost humility.

The other was a man gayly decked out. He wore a richly embroidered skin across his shoulders and a necklace of gaudy shells. He had a kind of mace in his hand. The lordly manner in which he carried his head indicated extreme pride and importance.

"Why," said Dave, backing into the gloomy depths of the cave, "that is the same dress the man wore who was the great priest of the tribe when I was on the Windjammers' Island the first time."

There seemed to be no doubt but that Dave was back on the old stamping-ground of Pat Stoodles. He was not at all sorry for this. It was the destination of the Swallow. Perhaps the steamer had already reached it.

"Things are working easier for me than I had any right to expect," reflected Dave, "only I must keep out of the clutches of any of the natives till I locate my friends."

Dave got behind an obscure rock. From there he peered intently at the two men who now entered the cave; the one crawling on his hands and knees, the other maintaining still his lofty bearing of superiority.

Reaching the mat, the guide arose to his feet. He showed the greatest humility and respect in all that he did.

He made a gesture to have his visitor sit down to the feast. The latter shook his head in great disdain.

Then the evident resident of the cave groaned and wept and rolled all over on the ground as if in the deepest despair. In a mournful sing-song voice he seemed to make an appeal to his august visitor to grant some prayer.

The priest finally stamped his foot and spoke some quick words. The other arose. The priest, fixing a menacing eye upon him, advanced, and putting out a hand, tried to pull aside the garment which the man wore on the upper part of his body.

The poor wretch seemed frantic. He clung close to the garment, seeming especially anxious not to expose his back or shoulders.

The priest, however, managed to tear the front of the garment open. Then Dave half understood the situation from something he remembered to have heard Stoodles tell about on a previous occasion.

A peculiar mark, a circle inclosing a cross, was visible on the chest of the suppliant.

"I know what that means," mused Dave. "They brand their criminals, drive them away, and if they ever approach the tribe again, they burn them alive. That is the outcast brand. Stoodles told me so when he was on this island with me."

The refugee cowered with shame. Then he kicked aside some of the dishes of the feast which his august visitor had spurned.

"I'm glad of that," thought Dave. "Now he won't be likely to notice that I have been trespassing."

The outcast went to a sort of shelf in the cave. He came back, poising a small earthen crock in his hand.

He began a quick talk to the priest in a louder, more assured tone. The latter suddenly changed his manner. His eyes sparkled. He looked eager and excited.

The outcast seemed to be giving a most glowing description of the contents of the little crock. Dave tried to follow his meaning.

"He is saying," translated Dave to himself, "that he has great quantities of whatever the crock contains--lots of it, heaps of it--I see. Now he has interested the priest. He is offering to buy his citizenship back into the tribe, that looks sure. Ah, he is showing what he has in the crock. Gracious!"

Dave forgot all prudence. He was so interested that he slipped out from hiding to gaze at the contents of the crock, now poured out rapidly by the outcast upon the food mat.

Fortunately the two men were equally engrossed. What the outcast had poured out of the crock were half a hundred or more pure gold coins!

CHAPTER XVIII

THE OUTCAST'S SECRET

The young ocean diver had a right to be astonished and interested. The first moment his eyes landed on the coins the outcast had exhibited, he felt sure they were part of the ocean treasure.

They were similar in size to the bulk of the pieces brought up from the ocean bed in the diving bell. They looked the same at a distance. Besides, where on this rarely visited island would the native get such a hoard except from the treasure heap?

The priest gathered up a lot of the coins. They manifestly pleased him. He laughed with glee and clinked them musically together in his hands.

Then he seemed to ask the outcast a great many questions. He stamped his feet as the latter appeared to evade direct answers.

"It's plain," said the anxiously watchful Dave, "those coins came from our stolen store. This native knows where it is."

Dave thought this a great discovery. From the way the outcast pointed Dave decided the bulk of the treasure was at a distance somewhere.

"I don't believe he has told the priest where," Dave surmised. "He seems bargaining to have the outcast edict removed, then he will pay a much greater amount. That's the way all this jabbering looks. Ah, they have come to an agreement."

The priest had become very gracious now. He pointed, too, in his rapid talk as if agreeing to return to the royal village and acted as if some proposal was to be made to the native king.

"I hope I can get out of here before they bring any more people," thought Dave. "I can't do it just now, though, that is sure."

The priest went away. The outcast began to array himself in new apparel. He grinned and chuckled and acted as if delighted. Dave figured out that he had bought his pardon.

Clearing the mat the native sat down in its center, first surrounding himself with a variety of native weapons.

"He is going to receive his company in state," decided Dare. "I simply couldn't get past him without being seen. He is heavily armed, too. Well, I'll have to wait patiently and watch out for my chance to escape."

One hour went by, two hours. Dave did not dare to stir from the covert in the cave where he crouched. Once the idea was suggested to his mind of overcoming the native who possessed a secret of such importance to him. The next moment, however, he saw how foolish this would be. Even if he succeeded, what could he do with the man, on his hands alone, not knowing the whereabouts of his friends, and his captive speaking a language he could not understand?

Dave was thinking over all these things when there came a sudden climax to the situation.

Without warning a dozen armed natives dashed past him with echoing yells.

It was patent to Dave that these men, apprized by the priest, had been instructed to steal into the cave by another entrance than the front one known to them and seize the outcast.

It looked as if the law of the island would not allow the king to treat on any terms whatever with an outcast. All the poor fellow's negotiations, therefore, seemed to have gone for naught. He must have realized treachery. He must have guessed that he would now be taken to the king as a captive, his secret tortured out of him, and the voice of the populace might demand that he be burned alive.

At all events he acted with acute alarm. He was on his feet in an instant. Dave saw him clear the entrance to the cave in a flash. The men who had burst so quickly upon the scene dashed out after him.

Dave could not help running to the entrance of the cave to see how things turned out. The fugitive had gone west away from the coast. Dave saw him far outdistance his pursuers. Darts and spears were hurled after him, but they all missed him. He finally disappeared into a grove, and distance shut out his pursuers as well.

Dave seized his spear and started promptly in the direction of the sea. In his brief survey from the heights he had made out the high plateau which he and Stoodles and Bob Vilett had once crossed in joining their friends on the other side of the island.

"It's due north, and it looks to be only about ten miles distant," calculated Dave. "I know that from the plateau we could see all over the island. If I could reach it, and the Swallow has arrived, I certainly could make her out. Yes, I must try to get to the plateau."

Dave used due haste in descending the cliff by the route he had come. He had the idea in his mind of trying to mend up the yawl on the beach. Then he would wait for dark and skirt the coast in the direction of the plateau.

He was glad when he got down to the shore bluffs. He planned how he would fix the hole in the side of the yawl and make some oars.

"I will make an inspection of the boat," he thought, going towards it across the beach. "I did not notice it particularly, and maybe it isn't much damaged."

The yawl lay keel upwards, as it had landed with him and as he had left it earlier in the morning.

As he got nearer he saw that several boards were badly sprung. They were, however, all above the waterline.

"I think I can manage to make it seaworthy for a little cruise," said Dave. "Wonder if she is damaged inside."

Dave stooped, put his hand under the side of the yawl, and gave the boat a tremendous lift and a push.

Over she went, but to disclose a fact that gave Dave a decided shock.

Three natives had lain in hiding under the yawl. They arose simultaneously. Three spears were leveled at Dave, and he knew he was a prisoner.

CHAPTER XIX

A DAY OF ADVENTURES

The three spears held Dave in a circle. The spearsmen advanced them nearer and nearer till they hemmed Dave in dangerously. He had placed his own weapon on the ground while attending to the boat, so he was entirely unarmed.

Dave could do nothing but quietly await the further action of his captors. They regarded him fiercely. Then there was a confab among them.

Two of them finally dropped their spears, leaving their companion to guard Dave. They went to the nearest bushes and secured some stringy vines of great strength.

They tied Dave's arms behind him. One of the men pointed west, in which direction the priest had gone. It seemed that the native village was located west.

A second of the trio dissented from the proposition made. He pointed down the shore a bit and talked volubly. Then the two went away, giving some directions to Dave's guard.

The latter, prodding Dave with the spear, made him go towards the shore bluffs. He forced him up an incline. There he secured a thick flexible vine, passed it through Dave's arms, and tied the other end around a tree.

He then threw himself on the ground and reclined there lazily.

From where he was Dave could look down the beach. He comprehended that the savages had come across the yawl and had probably seen his footmarks. They had calculated he would return and had hidden under the boat. Now, judging from the actions of the two natives down the beach, they were hunting for other footmarks.

At least it looked so to Dave. They seemed to locate some disturbance in the sand like a trail. They followed it up this course, which took them finally out of view of Dave.

Dave's guard reclined at the edge of the bluff, looking out at the sea. His spear lay beside him.

"I wish he would go to sleep," thought Dave. "With time given I'd bargain to get free from these flimsy bonds, if I had to gnaw through this big vine with my teeth."

The native, however, had no idea of going to sleep. He turned regularly about every two minutes to look at his captive.

Suddenly Dave saw the man start to rise up as if in great alarm. A look of horror was in his gleaming eyes. With a yell he toppled backwards. The amazed Dave saw him roll down the bluff incline. The native turned over and over, his head struck a great rock in the way with a fearful click. The blood flew from the wound and deluged the native's face and he lay like one dead, his body suspended over a bent sapling.

"Why," exclaimed the startled Dave, "what made him do that? Mercy!"

A lithe, sinuous form cut the air, coming from the thick shrubbery just back of Dave. It landed where the native had sat. Dave understood now. It was a panther.

His blood ran cold as the animal, disappointed of its expected prey, turned quickly, facing him. From former experiences on the island Dave knew that he confronted a foe dangerous and bloodthirsty in the extreme.

The native panther was feared by the natives greatly. It was a small animal, but ferocious to a degree and enormously strong in forefeet and teeth.

Dave, bound, unarmed, felt himself completely at the mercy of the animal. He shrank back, naturally, as it began to describe a semicircle. It crept low to the ground, uttering a harsh, hissing snarl. Its eyes were fixed intently on its intended victim.

Dave watched the fatal circle narrow. The panther came to a pause, a crouch. It shot up from the ground.

Dave had prepared for this first onset. He realized, however, that, helpless as he was, his agility could not eventually save him.

The youth made a leap as the panther sprang at him. Through a remarkable circumstance Dave's rush drew the big vine out. The panther met it coming up, was caught across the breast, and was sent hurtling back violently.

It fell to the ground, Dave ran at it. He ventured boldly, for the chances of escape were desperate. Dave delivered one kick at the prostrate animal. His foot partly landed in its gaping mouth.

"It's incredible!" cried Dave.

He was lost in wonderment. That resolute kick had worked marvels. As Dave looked at the ground he saw several teeth there and a trail of blood. Their owner had rolled back and had gone over the bluff as the native Had gone, uttering several frightful snarls.

"Will it come back again?" panted Dave. "A surprising adventure--I can hardly realize it. Yes, it is returning--no, human voices. Men, mates!" shouted Dave, "this way, this way!"

With anxious heart elate Dave had caught the voice of more than one person. Then a word in English, and he recognized the voice of Daley.

"Hello, where are you?" responded Daley's tones, their owner beating his way through the dense foliage.

"Young Fearless! We've found him," he cried, staring hard. "Turned up again, eh, lad?"

"I'm mighty glad you have," said Dave rapidly. "What, the three of you, and safe and sound?" he added, as two others joined their leader.

"We were looking for you," announced Daley. "Here, one of you has a pocket knife. Cut the lad loose."

"You were looking for me?" repeated Dave wonderingly.

"To be sure," nodded Daley. "We washed ashore last night all safe and trim, as you see."

"Yes, but not near here, for I looked for a trace of you," said Dave.

"No, it must have been a good ten miles to the south, lad. We made this way, and saw those natives get under that boat. We were unarmed and hid. When those two up the beach left you in charge of the fellow here, we rounded into the bluffs and searched for you. Where is the fellow, anyhow?"

Dave narrated what had taken place. Daley looked pretty serious.

"We're in a nest of them, it seems," he remarked, taking up the spear belonging to Dave's guard. "Come on, mates; let's make a tight run for it while the coast is still clear of them."

Daley's plan was a simple one and Dave allowed it to prevail. It was to get north as fast and far as they could before they were discovered by more natives.

"They're thick back of the coast, just hereabouts," said Daley. "We heard their yells several times in our jaunt down shore, and saw several of them. Keep in the cover of the bluff, and let us try to round that cape yonder. From what I remember here before, the cyclone pretty well cleaned out the north end of the island."

"That is true," said Dave, "and the natives probably shun it on that account."

Their progress was very satisfactory. The cape that Daley had alluded to was reached about two hours later.

It presented a sheer high wall to the sea and gave a fine view of the island for miles around. It was wooded to within about fifty feet of the edge.

They were all terribly tired out and badly torn with thorns and brambles. As they came out into clear space, Daley and his companions threw themselves down on the ground, nearly exhausted.

Dave, starting to follow their example, paused, uttered a great shout, and ran to the sheer edge of the cliff.

"Hello, there--what's doing, mate?" challenged Daley, in some wonder.

"See! see! see!" cried Dave, pointing down at the sea with shining eyes--"the Swallow!"

CHAPTER XX

ON BOARD THE "SWALLOW"

"Captain Broadbeam, come here, please."

"Why, lad, what's the matter?"

Bob Vilett had spoken in a way that might well have excited the surprise of the commander of the steamer.

For over ten minutes Bob had stood at the side, gazing through a spyglass landwards. Now of a sudden the glass dropped in his nerveless hand. Bob began to tremble, and he had called to the friendly captain like one in distress.

"Those natives up to some more high jinks?" said Broadbeam, coming up to Bob.

"No, no, captain! Look--look! Quick, captain!"

"Toplights and gaffsails, what's this now?" demanded Broadbeam, as Bob extended the glass, looking pale and agitated.

"Look at the high cape cliff, captain," urged Bob. "See if I'm mistaken."

"Dave Fearless!" fairly roared the old sea veteran the minute he put the glass to his eyes.

"You are sure, captain?" cried Bob, in great excitement.

The captain had been staggered at his surprising first view through the spyglass. Now he looked again.

"Dave! Ah, a glad sight," he went on. "Some men with him--look like sailors. Fearless! Amos Fearless! Where is he? Old friend, your son is alive!"

Those of the crew in sight and hearing stared quite wonderingly at their captain. They had rarely seen him so moved as when he ran towards the cabin, shouting the name of his friend.

"What is that?" said the old diver, coming up the cabin stairs.

"Dave is alive."

"My son alive," cried Amos Fearless, turning white, and in a momentary weakness holding to a rail for support.

"Yes, he is--ashore there."

"Oh, are you sure?"

"Go look for yourself. Hurrah!"

Captain Broadbeam was beside himself with genuine gladness.

He clamped his big paw of a hand across his old friend's arm and fairly dragged him across the deck.

"Yes, it's Dave," cried the happy father, taking a look through the spyglass. Then he handed it back to Bob Vilett. The old diver turned his face away. It was wet with tears of thankfulness and joy.

Captain Broadbeam moved about the deck too excited to stand still.

"I felt it in my bones! Didn't I say it all along?" he spoke. "Didn't I stick to it that a lad born to the sea would find a way out of it? Below there, Adams," he hailed to the engineer, "how's she working?"

"Bad, sir; mortal bad," reported the engineer.

There was something serious the matter with the Swallow. There had been since the night previous.

Dave Fearless had not been missed from the ship until that morning. Then they had searched everywhere for him. It became patent after an investigation that he had been swept overboard.

There was little chance to look for him. The storm that had given Dave and his refugee friends, Daley and the others, such a terrible experience, had dealt the stanch little steamer a severe blow.

There had been times during the tempest when the Swallow was thrown about like an eggshell in the grasp of a giant. She was cast on her beam-ends more than once.

The steamer outrode the storm just in time. She could not have stood another hour of that terrible tossing about and wrenching.

With a grave face Adams had called Captain Broadbeam down into the engine room to see the damage that had been done.

The engine was fairly out of commission. One driving rod was bent badly, some of the minor mechanism was clear out of gear.

"It's land and a quiet harbor mighty quick, sir," reported the experienced engineer, "or trouble if another storm strikes us on the open sea."

"You are right, Adams," said the captain, after due investigation. "We must make land somehow, somewhere. The Swallow is badly crippled."

"You see, sir," observed Adams, "I have rigged up a temporary makeshift for a driving rod. It may give out at any moment under strain. If we can work our way easy like and crawl to harborage, in a few days with some blacksmithing we might forge or rig up some new parts."

It was just after this that land was discovered, and Stoodles came into a general consultation as an authority that they were surely approaching the Windjammers' Island.

Their former experience in these same waters was of value now. Adams advised that they get close to the shore and line it, looking for a temporary harbor.

Bob Vilett had a valuable suggestion to make. He was in a pretty gloomy mood over the unknown fate of his chum, for whom they had spent two hours with all the small boats out.

Bob, however, had to stick to his duty. It nearly broke his heart to witness the prostration of the old diver, but as he thought of something, he went to the captain.

"When we were here before, captain," he said, "you remember the natural harbor where we found the old derelict vessel?"

"Why," said Broadbeam, "the very thing. Thanks for the suggestion, lad. If we can reach that spot we are safe from any bother from the natives here and from any storm that may come up. Tell Adams."

The Swallow had been discovered by the natives about an hour later. These came to the beach in several places. They made a great ado. Whole processions came into view. At one place they brought down a covered platform borne by four men. Upon this platform was a great earthen pot filled with some smoking material.

"What are they up to, Pat?" the captain asked Stoodles.

"Begorra, it's the ould magic spell of their high-priests to send us bad luck," answered the Irishman.

The various incantations of the natives went on nearly under the eyes of those on board of the Swallow for some time. Then the visitations to the beach ceased. It was now about half an hour later that Bob Vilett had discovered Dave Fearless on the cape cliff where the young diver and his three companions had just arrived.

While Mr. Fearless was gazing anxiously ashore and Bob was tracing every movement of his distant chum through the spyglass, Captain Broadbeam was giving quick orders to his men.

A boat was to go ashore at once and a signal given from the deck of the Swallow that Dave would understand.

"Don't delay, my friends," the excited Stoodles kept urging the sailors. "Let us get into action before my former subjects come into sight again."

All was ready, boat, men, and weapons, to start to the succor of Dave, when Bob Vilett uttered a shout of dismay.

"Oh, captain," he cried, running up to the commander of the Swallow, "it's too late."

"How's this? What do you mean?" demanded the captain.

He snatched the glass from Bob's hand and took a look himself. Then he uttered a hollow groan.

Dave and the others were still visible on the cliff, but over a hundred natives had suddenly swarmed about them.

As he looked, the captain saw these surround Dave and the others. They were seized, bound, and carried off into the forest before his very eyes.

CHAPTER XXI

THE ISLAND HARBOR

The great joy that the friends of Dave Fearless had experienced, at discovering him almost in reach, now gave way to great anxiety as he seemed lost to them again.

Bob Vilett was summoned to the engine room by his superior. Amos Fearless went back to the cabin, looking dejected and sad.

Captain Broadbeam fumed secretly. He paced the deck rapidly, going through considerable mental perturbation.

Pat Stoodles saw the expedition ashore abandoned.

He knew the captain's fiery moods and kept out of the way for a spell. When the Swallow turned her head directly north he approached Broadbeam.

"It's on your way you'd be going, captain dear?" mildly observed Stoodles.

"Don't you see I am?" challenged Broadbeam petulantly.

"It's disturbed ye are, I see," said the plausible Irishman. "Ochone, ye may well be. Wirra-wirra! that fine broth of a boy, Dave Fearless, abandoned to his fate. Deserted by his friends."

"Who's abandoning him, who's deserting him?" flamed out the captain.

"That's it. I was asking your honor," said Stoodles innocently. "Of course ye have plans to assist the lad. I know the island. Wasn't I their king once on a time? Make me your confidant, captain dear. What's your plans?"

"I'll show those bloodthirsty villains soon," declared Broadbeam, shaking his ponderous fist at the island. "I'm going around to anchor in the cove at the northwest end of the island."

"I see," nodded Stoodles thoughtfully. "A foine spot. And then, captain?"

"Every man aboard armed to the teeth, and let those savages look out. My duty is first to my ship. When I have her safe at anchorage it's Dave Fearless, first, last, and all the time."

"Captain," observed Stoodles enthusiastically, "you're a jewel!"

Stoodles went apart by himself, smiling and apparently intensely satisfied. He seemed planning something all the rest of the time it took to go about one-third around the island.

The sheltered cove into which the Swallow finally ran was located at a remote and unfrequented part of the island.

It was here that on a former occasion a derelict had lain shut in, undiscovered for a long time, by great forests and guarded by steep cliffs towards the sea.

The ravages of a great cyclone were visible here and there as the Swallow neared its port. The steamer ran under a network of vines that hung like a curtain across the front of this singular cove.

The first thing done, once a permanent mooring was made, was to carry a portable forge ashore. Adams, the engineer, selected two of the crew who had some knowledge of blacksmithing.

"We'll have the Swallow in taut trim inside of three days, captain," Adams promised.

"Good," nodded the commander. "I leave it to you. Now then, to adopt some plan to reach Dave Fearless."

The boatswain came up and touched his cap respectfully.

"What is it, Drake?" inquired Broadbeam.

"That man, Gerstein."

"Well, what about him?"

"Uneasy, sir. I've been watching him closely. I found a package of food and a knife and a pistol hidden under his bunk this morning."

"You did, eh?" muttered the captain thoughtfully. "Preparing to bolt, you think?"

"I know it."

"Won't do," advised Broadbeam tersely. "Lock him up."

"In irons, captain?"

"No, the hold storeroom is safe and sound. Put him there. We mustn't let the man escape until we know what he knows."

Captain Broadbeam had a long talk with Amos Fearless. He decided that early the next morning they would make up a strong party, well armed, and march on the native town of the Windjammers.

"Come in here, my friends," said the captain to Pat Stoodles and Bob Vilett, at the end of his talk with Mr. Fearless.

He then told them of his decision. Stoodles did not say much. Bob was pleased and eager to start on the foray.

"I hope we shall be in time," sighed Dave's father anxiously. "Those natives may even now have killed their captives."

"You're wrong there, Mr. Fearless," declared Stoodles, with confidence. "Listen, sir. Wasn't I once king of that fine lot of natives? Don't I know their ways? Very well, my friends, if you will look at the moon to-night you will find it on the lasht quarter. The Windjammers never kill a prisoner except from a new moon up to a full moon."

"Is that true, Pat?" asked Captain Broadbeam.

"True to the letther, sir--who knows betther than I, who have had experience? Yes, sir, they won't harm the lad or his comrades for over a week at the least, unless in a fight or an accident. Those natives who came out on the big rock had come there to cast another spell on the ship. Dave couldn't get away seawards without dropping into the sea. He couldn't fight half the tribe. He's given in quietly, as we saw, sir. They'll shut him up; that's all for the present. We'll get him out; that's all for the future. Now, captain dear, I've got something of a favor to ask of you."

"All right, Pat, what is it?"

"Don't march down on the Windjammers. I've said nothing against your plans until the right moment."

"Well?" asked Broadbeam.

"I've a betther plan than your own to offer. Listen, sir--the most you can muster is half a dozen able men."

"A dozen, fully."

"And leave the ship unguarded? All right, captain, call it a dozen. What then? You march on a thousand natives. No, no, sir," said Stoodles, shaking his head solemnly, "they would wipe you off the face of the earth, first move. Don't be foolish, sir. Let me thry."

"Try what?"

"To rescue me young friend, Dave Fearless. Captain, you remember how I hocused them and came it over them when you were here before?"

"Yes, Pat, I have a very vivid memory of some of your whimsical doings," answered the captain, smiling.

"Then one favor, captain: loan me Bob Vilett and a few traps I need. Give me two days to bring back Dave Fearless."

Amos Fearless looked anxious, the captain undecided.

"Do it, captain," urged Bob Vilett eagerly. "I have great faith in Mr. Stoodles."

The captain reflected seriously for a moment or two. He glanced at the old diver. The latter nodded. Anything that might affect his son's welfare appealed to him strongly.

"Do it, then," said Captain Broadbeam, "only, remember, you two take your own risks."

CHAPTER XXII

THE HOUSE OF TEARS

"Hooray!" said Pat Stoodles, as soon as they were out of the presence of Captain Broadbeam and the diver.

"All right now, eh?" insinuated Bob curiously.

"Shure I am. Now, my friend, I've done you the honor of selecting you to go with me. You're willing?"

"Try me," cried Bob stanchly.

"The first thing," said Stoodles, "is to see Doctor Barrell."

"What! You're not thinking of taking him with us?" cried Bob.

"Not at all," responded Stoodles, "but I do want to take with me something he has got."

"And what's that, Pat?" asked Bob.

"His phonnygraph."

"Aha, I see," cried Bob, grinning. "The time you visited your subjects before you worked on their superstitious fears by rubbing phosphorus on your face. This time----"

"I'm reckoning on giving them a spaach, lad. Lave that end to me. What I want you to do is to make another of those paper balloons you sent up into the air the Fourth of July out at sea."

"Sure," said Bob; "a dozen, if you like."

"No, make two, for one might get disabled. Have you any of the fireworks left?"

"No, but I can make almost any kind of a sizzer with powder and fuses the purser will let me have."

"All right," approved Stoodles. "I may want to send up a balloon at the proper moment. If I do, I want it to send out lots of sparks when it gets aloft."

"You leave all that to me, Mr. Stoodles," said Bob. "I'll guarantee a perfect job."

"It's all for Dave's sake, lad, so I know you will," declared Stoodles.

The eccentric but loyal Irishman now went to the stateroom occupied by Doctor Barrell.

"Docther," he said, entering the presence of the old scientist, "I'd be telling you something."

Doctor Barrell was very busy examining some seaweed specimens he had fished up in the cove, but he graciously received the visitor, who was quite a favorite with him.

"Speak right out, Mr. Stoodles," he said.

Pat narrated his plans in behalf of Dave Fearless. Doctor Barrell was interested.

"And how can I help you?" he inquired, when Stoodles had finished talking.

"Docther dear, it's the loan of your phonnygraph I'd be wanting."

Doctor Barrell looked serious. He had a remarkably fine phonograph outfit, receiver and transmitter attachments, and all up to date.

This he greatly valued, for he was accustomed to talk his scientific deductions into a receiver, preserving the records for future reference when he got back to the United States.

"Tell me about what you want to reach, Mr. Stoodles," said the kindly old fellow, "and I'll see if I can fix you out properly."

Stoodles explained his scheme. After that he was shut up with the doctor for several hours. When he rejoined Bob his face was beaming.

"It's all right, lad," he reported. "Ah, but a wise old fellow is Docther Barrell. It'll be amazing what we are going to do to the natives."

It was just before dusk that evening when Stoodles and Bob left the Swallow. They each carried a good-sized parcel. The captain had seen to it that they were furnished with small-arms.

The ship's yawl took them out of the cove and landed them about five miles down shore, the boatswain in charge.

"It's understood, then," said Drake, "that we be here again with the boat at six, twelve, and six to-morrow?"

"If we're alive and well," answered Stoodles, "you'll find us on hand on one of those three occasions."

"That has saved us a long, hard tramp," said Bob, shouldering his load as they started inland.

"Two-thirds of the journey, lad, if the native town is where I think it is," answered Stoodles. "Now, everything depends on getting to the town and into it without being seen."

"Yes," assented Bob, "and it may prove a hard task."

"Not if you do exactly as I say," declared Stoodles. "Just follow me. I know all the short cuts."

The journey was not a pleasant one. There was no beaten path to follow. They had to breast their way at places through whole acres of thorny bushes. At other places they had some steep rocks to climb.

They rested frequently. It was about two hours later when Stoodles pressed through the last canes of a great brake with an expression of intense satisfaction.

"The hardest part of our tramp is over and done with, lad," he announced.

"That's good news," said Bob, who was pretty tired.

"Now you rest here till I get up into a tree and take a peep in a certain direction."

Stoodles selected a high, lonely tree near at hand, and was soon up among its loftiest branches. He came down speedily.

"It's all right, Bob," he stated. "A mile more and we will be at the edge of the town."

"The new town?" asked Bob. "The old one was destroyed by the cyclone, you know."

"Yes, the new town. It's not far away. I can tell by the lights."

It was now, as they reached a moderately level plateau, that they found paths evidently used regularly by the natives.

One of these lay right through a large field of flowers that resembled poppies. These appeared to be under cultivation.

"What's the flower garden for?" asked Bob.

"These are the royal flowers, lad," explained the Irishman. "They use them for royal celebrations and funerals. Bad cess to it! If we should be found here by the natives."

"Why?" inquired Bob.

"Taboo. No one is allowed here except the women who give their life to tending to the flowers, unless by direct permission of the native king."

"Well," observed Bob quizzically, "you had ought to be able to get a free pass, seeing that you was king once."

Stoodles chuckled as if some pleasant idea was suggested to his mind.

"I'll be king again," he observed. "I've got to be. 'Tis only for an hour maybe, but Dave Fearless and I want to make that ten thousand dollars."

"What ten thousand dollars?" asked Bob eagerly, as Stoodles paused in some confusion.

"You'd better ask Dave that," suggested Stoodles.

"Oh, I know what you are hinting at," said Bob. "It's some schemes concerning those two boxes Dave got at Minotaur Island."

"Ah, is it now?" said Stoodles, with an expression of vacancy on his face.

"I am sure it is," persisted Bob, "and I know what is in those boxes."

"Hear him! Well, well!" commented Stoodles.

"It's a little printing outfit. Pat, what are you and Dave going to mix up these natives with a printing outfit for? Won't you tell me?"

"Lad," pronounced Stoodles solemnly, "that is a dark and deadly saycret for the present."

Bob had to be satisfied with this. He followed his guide in silence. Stoodles halted.

"Do you see that old building yonder?" he asked of his companion.

"Yes," nodded Bob, curiously regarding a rude broad hut occupying an elevated space just beyond the flower field.

"Well, take my bundle. That's it. Now don't sthir till I come out. Crouch down among these bushes. I've got to get into that building to make my plans good."

"What is it, anyhow?" inquired Bob.

"They call it the House of Tears," was the rather singular reply of Stoodles.

CHAPTER XXIII

READY FOR ACTION

"I wonder what he has gone in there for?" thought Bob Vilett, as Stoodles disappeared in the direction of the House of Tears.

Bob had not long to wait. Stoodles came back as silently as he had gone.

"Aisy, lad!" he warned. "There's people about."

"I don't see any."

"In the pagoda yonder. There's a dozen or more mourners, all widows."

"Oh, I understand why it is called the House of Tears now," said Bob.

"I was in on them with a stumble. By good luck the lights were low for one thing, and they were all given up to their groaning and mourning. Well, I got these two, anyhow."

"Two what?" interrogated Bob. "Oh, I see," he added, as he made out two curious garments in the hands of his companion.

Spreading one out at a time, Stoodles showed Bob what they were.

"Any royal mourner," he explained, "wears one of these constantly for a full month after the death of a relative. They are taboo all that time. They must not be hindered. They are free to go where they choose."

"Good," commented Bob, "they'll help us out, then, won't they?"

"Yes. Get into this one, lad; it's the shortest," said Stoodles.

The garment was of one piece, covering a person from head to foot. Its top was a cap with holes for the eyes only.

When the two friends were arrayed in the garments they presented queer figures. Each carried his bundle under its ample folds.

The next half-hour was an interesting one for Bob. He simply followed Stoodles. Somehow he could not help but have confidence in the whimsical old fellow. For one thing, Stoodles certainly knew his ground well from experience. Besides that, he had been successful in carrying his point when he had before visited the native town when they were marooned on the island by the Raven crowd.

It was now past midnight. As they progressed Bob could see that they were nearing a lot of habitations.

For the most part the native village made up of squalid-looking huts.

Here and there, however, were some more pretentious structures. So far they had not met a single person.

"The palace, the home of the king, that same," said Stoodles, as they paused near the largest building they had yet seen.

"What's the programme?" asked Bob.

"You see that little pagoda attached behind?"

Bob nodded affirmatively.

"That is the council temple. I must get in there."

"It looks easy," said Bob. "Those sides of matting are not hard to break through."

"No, but the place is guarded day and night by as many as six natives," explained Stoodles. "They sleep all around the curtained daïs that holds the royal throne. Lad, I must get to that throne."

"All right," said Bob. "And what am I to do?"

"Listen very carefully. You see that big rock in the center of the square yonder?"

"With a great bowl-like thing at the top of it?" asked Bob.

"Yes. That is the public tribune, or place where the king's messengers make announcements to the people. That big bowl is filled with a perfumed water once a year, and the people pass under it while the high priest of the tribe throws a few drops over each of them."

"Go ahead," said Bob, "this is kind of interesting."

"Now then," pursued Stoodles, "I have planned out just what I want to have you do. Don't make any miss, lad."

"I'll make no miss--you just instruct me," said Bob.

"You are to climb up into that bowl. It's perfectly dry now. It's deep enough to hold you and all your traps. In just an hour you fire off a revolver, its full round of charges. Get your balloon ready. I'll hand you up the phonnygraph. Start it up--that's all."

"But what's going to come of it all?"

"You will soon see that."

"And what am I to do when the performance is over?" demanded Bob.

"I'll see that you are properly taken care of," declared Stoodles.

"All right," said Bob. "I suppose you know what you are about, but it's a pretty elaborate programme you are laying out."

"Oh, I know how to hocus these superstitious people, that's all," said Stoodles lightly. "I've done it before, you know."

Stoodles took Bob over to the public tribune. Everybody in the village seemed to be asleep. They were apparently unnoticed and undisturbed as they got the bundles up into the great bowl.

Bob climbed in after. Stoodles gave him a few last words of direction. Then he started off to carry out his own part of the programme.

The side of the great earthen bowl in which Bob now found himself was perforated all around the scalloped outer edges. Bob kept Stoodles in sight as long as he could by peering through one of these.

"He has gone in the direction of the royal council room," thought Bob. "This is a queer go. I wonder how it will turn out? In an hour, he said--all right."

Bob looked at his watch, flashing a match for the purpose. Then he arranged the various paraphernalia that were to take part in Pat Stoodles' programme.

He got the phonograph placed to suit him and ready for action at a moment's notice. Bob also prepared one of the small paper balloons so he could light the alcohol sponge on the wire on its bottom without igniting the tissue paper. A perforated asbestos globe he had himself designed, enabled him to do this with facility.

The native village slept. No sound broke the silence of the mystic midnight hour.

Bob again consulted his watch. The hour prescribed by Stoodles had passed.

"Everything must have worked smoothly with Pat," thought the young engineer. "I'm due to start the ball rolling all right. Here goes!"

CHAPTER XXIV

IN THE ROYAL PALACE

Bang, bang, bang, bang!

Such a vivid, unfamiliar racket had seemingly never before disturbed the native town of the Island Windjammers.

The whole settlement seemed to wake up at once. Bob Vilett was fairly startled at the result of his sharp rapid fusillade.

He had a heap to do, however, and he had no time to observe what was going on outside.

The balloon called first for Bob's attention. The shots alone had not directed the excited natives to the public tribune. The balloon, rising majestically, centered all eyes on that central meeting-place.

A hush of awe hung over the crowd. Bob started up the phonograph.

He did not know what the little machine was saying. He could only surmise that it was grinding out a speech from Stoodles. Loud and sonorous rang forth the tones of the fertile-minded Milesian.

Bob, venturing to peer from the bowl that encased him, was truly amazed.

Most of the crowd that had gathered stood perfectly still. Some of the more superstitious, at a sight of the strange balloon, had fallen prostrate in terror.

The speech now coming forth from the phonograph had a wonderful effect. It seemed to transfix the people. There was not a murmur, a stir, until the last word had issued from the phonograph. Then babel broke loose, the spot was deserted by magic. Men shouted, yelled, ran over each other in a pell-mell dash in the direction of the king's palace.

Bob tried hard to guess out the situation. He could only reason that the speech in the old familiar tones of their former king, coming from an unseen, mysterious source, had duly impressed the people. The shots, the balloon now dropping a vivid trail of sparks far aloft, had added to the general effect.

"I suppose I'm due to wait here until further orders," ruminated Bob. "I'd like to know what is going on in the palace, though."

Bob got restive thinking about this. The commotion and excitement around the palace were momentarily increasing.

"I can be of no further use here," thought Bob. "I don't see how Stoodles is going to get me out of here without giving the natives a hint as to my agency in sending up the fireworks and playing the phonograph. I'm going to get out of this; yes, I am."

Bob was an impatient, persistent sort of a fellow. Having made up his mind to leave his hiding-place, he promptly succeeded in getting out of the bowl and down onto the ground.

"I'm safe in this outlandish garment Pat gave me," reasoned Bob, securing his belongings under its folds. "I'm going to join the procession and see what is going on."

Bob pressed on the outskirts of the howling, excited mob that surrounded the palace. Then he edged his way in among them.

He found out that the robe he wore was indeed "taboo." People made way for him. Thus proceeding, Bob got finally right up to the little pagoda that Stoodles had designated to him as the royal council room.

Its entrance was choked and crowded with natives trying to enter.

Bob kept working his way farther and farther along. At last he squeezed past two great greasy sentinels and saw Pat Stoodles.

The Milesian sat on a heap of skins next to a throne raised on a daïs. Upon the throne itself sat a dusky native. Bob decided, from his manner and the deference with which he was treated by the others, that he must be the king.

All around were savages, more or less decorated in a way not common with the simple natives.

These persons, Bob knew, must comprise the nobility and the high-priests of the tribe.

Stoodles was speaking volubly, and seemed to take his honors and the situation in an easy, familiar way.

Of course Bob could not understand the native tongue, but he quickly saw that in some way the shrewd Milesian had got things on a most friendly basis with the tribe and its leaders.

"I wish I could get nearer and attract his attention," thought Bob. "I want him to know I have left the public square. I'll venture it. Pat!"

The next moment Bob Vilett was sorry he had spoken. He had not realized that to utter a word unbidden in the royal council room without royal permission was to court the severest public censure.

Four guards grabbed him up in a moment. All those around the royal daïs looked towards the present center of commotion in amazement.

Bob struggled in the grasp of his fierce captors, but was hampered by the bundles he carried. Suddenly one of the guards discovered he had shoes on. They tore away the garment encircling him. Some hurried words were called out to the king. In stern tones that monarch responded.

Bob could tell from the menacing manner of the guards that he was being borne away to punishment.

"Stoodles! Pat Stoodles!" he shouted at the top of his voice.

"Aha!" he heard Stoodles exclaim, and then the Milesian added words in the native language.

The guards looked amazed. They received a new order from the king. Bob was carried to the foot of the daïs.

"Make a bow," suggested Stoodles, and Bob did so. Stoodles no longer wore the mourning garb. That on Bob was riddled.

"It's all roight. I was soon coming after you," said Stoodles. "Everything is fixed."

"How fixed?" inquired the wondering Bob.

"Don't you see," insinuated the smiling Stoodles, with a gracious wave of his hand, "nothing is too good for me or my friends?"

"How did you work it?" asked Bob, feeling perfectly safe and easy now.

"That phonnygraph recited a great spaach of mine. It told the people that they would find their old king, myself, seated on the throne here. Why, lad, when they did find me I could have ousted the new king in a minute. I was magnanimous, though. I only asked some information. I told him he could keep his throne in peace."

The king and his counselors stared at the twain as they conversed, but did not interrupt.

"Whisht, lad!" continued Stoodles, with a chuckle. "They've given me some great information."

"What is it?" asked Bob.

"The Raven crowd are alive. I have found out where they are."

"Good!" said Bob.

"I have threatened all kinds of fire gods and cyclone demons unless they set Dave Fearless free."

"Will they?" asked Bob eagerly.

"Shure they will. He'll be here safe and sound in a few minutes. There's the guards they sent for him now."

Some natives bearing spears came hurrying into the room. There arose a great excited jabber. Stoodles rose up in manifest disappointment.

"What about Dave?" persisted Bob.

"Ochone!" cried Pat Stoodles. "Dave has spoiled everything!"

"Spoiled everything?" repeated Bob.

"Yes; Dave has escaped."

CHAPTER XXV

THE CAPTIVES

"Mr. Daley, you are a brave man."

"Glad of the compliment, Dave Fearless. I hope I deserve it."

"You certainly do," asserted Dave warmly. "But where are Jones and Lewis?"

Daley, who had flushed with pleasure at the handsome compliment bestowed by the young friend he was learning to like and respect, scowled and muttered angrily at this allusion to the companions who had been captured with them by the natives on the cape bluff.

"They're cowards, that's what they are," cried Daley angrily, "the miserable villains."

"Well, I hope they got away safely, anyhow," said Dave simply.

"They don't deserve it," growled Daley. "Now then, lad, so far so good. But what next?"

"That's so," remarked Dave Fearless. "What next, indeed?"

It was the second day after their capture. Dave and Daley were in a queer environment, to explain which it is necessary to go back to the hour when they were discovered on the cape bluff by the natives.

Their great joy at the discovery of the Swallow so near at hand off the island coast, had been quickly shadowed.

As Dave's anxious friends had seen through the spyglass from the deck of the steamer, the arrival of a large body of natives had put an end to the freedom of the young ocean diver and his companions. All four were surrounded and bound.

While some of the savages went on with their fetich ceremonies on the bluff to cast an evil spell on the Swallow, the others marched the captives to the native town.

There they were placed in a wretched hut, without any roof. The hut filled a cavity in the ground. About a dozen natives squatted on the surrounding level, and were thus enabled to keep the captives constantly in sight.

The rest of that day and the next passed in this irksome confinement. The prisoners were given food and water, but the great vigilance of their guards was not relaxed.

There was not the least opportunity afforded to escape.

When night came again, Daley and the others went to sleep. They had become disheartened. Dave, however, never gave up. Escape was constantly in his mind. His chance came at midnight.

Dave did not know it then, but Stoodles and Bob Vilett were responsible for the opportunity afforded.

Of a sudden, Dave caught the sounds of great commotion in the center of the native village, from which their prison place was quite remote.

Some men came running by, shouting loudly to the guards. Dave was amazed to see the last two of these spring to their feet in great excitement. They babbled like frightened monkeys. Then, with frantic yells, they dashed away towards the village.

It took Dave Fearless less than a minute to arouse his sleeping companions. It took less than another minute to show them that a golden opportunity for escape was presented.

It had not been a question of getting rid of their bonds at any time. These had grown loose from their twisting about during the day. It was the work of but a moment to cast them to the ground.

"There is not a single guard left," said Dave. "Something great and exciting is evidently happening at the native village. Work fast, men. We must get out of the enclosure some way quick as we can. Then a dash for the timber yonder."

Daley braced himself against the side wall of the enclosure. Dave mounted to his shoulders. As soon as he got safely over on the solid ground, Dave secured some poles. These he slanted down into the prison place. The others scrambled up them with agility and had soon joined him.

"What's that?" demanded Daley suddenly. "There it is again. No, gone. Something like a big fireball. The trees shut it out. Now then, Fearless, lead the way."

Daley had caught a momentary glimpse of the balloon Bob Vilett had sent aloft. Had Dave seen this, it might have suggested the near proximity of friends from the Swallow and have changed his plans.

As it was, he, like his companions, had only one thought in view--to get to a safe distance before the guards might return, discover their absence, and arouse the tribe to a general pursuit.

The refugees were most fortunate in their movements for the next few hours. Dave had struck out due west. They soon passed all signs of habitations.

It was two o'clock in the morning when they halted. The others lay down on the ground. Dave rested a few minutes. Then he arose and walked a short distance from the spot.

He was intent on studying their surroundings and learning what prospect lay beyond a sharp rise just in their course to the west.

The moon shone brightly, but by spells clouds occasionally crossed the sky. Dave had to wait for these fitful illuminations to pick his course.

Near to the top of the rise Dave halted, studied a slight glare, and then started on again with caution.

"A fire," he said. "Yes, I can smell smoke. Natives around a camp-fire? I guess that much. I must hurry back to the others and make back tracks double-quick."

Dave hastened along fast and recklessly. The sure proximity of enemies had startled him.

"What's this?" he gasped suddenly, lost his footing, took a header, and plunged into complete darkness.

CHAPTER XXVI

A THRILLING ADVENTURE

Dave had fallen down a hole covered with a thin network of branches and leaves. He knew it to be a trap, a pitfall, as he began his descent. There was a strong rancid smell about the spot, and the earth and the branches were thickly covered with grease.

Dave went shooting, feet first, down a smooth slant. He landed with a shock. Then he rebounded, lost his balance, and fell flat.

With a thrill he struck something moving, something that grunted, and tore away from him. It seemed covered with sharp, ugly bristles that had penetrated his hands like thorns.

Dave sprang to his feet in alarm. Fierce echoing grunts filled the place, a pit of considerable size. He quickly drew out a match and flared it.

"A wild boar," said Dave, and as he took in his situation he was swept off his feet with a new shock.

The momentary illumination had fully apprized Dave of his environment. The pit was a trap, its entrance scented and greased to attract victims.

A strong home-made rope was attached to a stake in its center. Its end was a loop. This loop now inclosed the neck of the boar, choking and imprisoning it. In fact, the fierce animal was fairly frantic.

The loop must have been placed in some way near to decoy food, tightening and securing its victim at a touch.

Now rushing around, the boar had swept Dave off his footing with the taut rope at which it struggled. It was upon him in an instant. Mad with pain and fright it tried to gore and crush him.

Dave managed to roll and squirm beyond its reach. Breathless and bewildered, he hurriedly drew out his pocket knife, opening its largest blade.

With blazing eyes the maddened animal made another rush at Dave. He went flat. Its tusk penetrated a double thickness of his clothing. It tugged at him, panting, grunting, squealing.

Snip-snip--Dave was all mixed up in the rope, almost helplessly at the mercy of the animal. He slashed out with the knife, but struck the rope instead of the boar.

The rope parted. Dave was dragged over the pit floor, his clothing firmly held by the spike-like tusk of the boar.

He had to go along, whether he would or not. Dave grasped one bristly ear of the boar.

"Whew!" he uttered, mind and body in such a turmoil that he could not realize what had happened till it was all over.

The boar, freed, had made a dash out of the pit. It seemed to Dave that it took some avenue of exit different to the slant down which he himself had tumbled into the pit.

At all events, he found himself in the open air, but borne along at a terrific rate of speed. He could hardly cling to the animal.

He let go his grasp entirely as the boar scaled a rise and toppled over. Dave, however, could not disengage his clothing. Then he was conscious of rolling over and over. The big animal seemed to fade from view in a swift flight. Dave's head struck something and he lost his senses.

When Dave came back to consciousness, there was no mistake as to his situation. A single glance enlightened him.

A dozen natives were working around a charcoal fire. They seemed to be hardening spear-heads, darts, and other weapons used by the Windjammers as weapons of war.

Near by was a square hut. Its door stood open, the only aperture it contained. Its top was flat and sunken, and leaning up against the sides of this parapet-like inclosure Dave noticed numberless weapons.

Dave lay flat on the ground, feet and hands both tied. The wild boar was nowhere in evidence. The natives were going on with their work.

"Weapon-makers," said Dave. "They seem to be finishing up their work, for the fire is going out."

Finally one of the men--there were four of them--finished holding a lot of spear-ends in the fire. He came and looked at Dave, discovered his eyes were open, and spoke some quick words to him.

Dave shook his head to indicate that he did not understand. A few minutes later all four men piled the various articles they had been burning upon a sort of litter.

They seemed about to carry this into the hut. Each took a corner of the litter.

Here something happened. Dave almost imagined himself in a dream, as he saw a swift form burst from some bushes near at hand.

It was Daley. He was armed with a great knotted club. Evidently he had been watching for just this opportunity to interest himself in behalf of his young friend and overpower his captors.

The four natives employed at the litter had no time or chance to defend themselves.

Whack! Whack! In turn two of them went flat with broken heads.

Whack! Whack! Their companions toppled over, and the litter fell to the ground.

"Up with you," roared the giant sailor, a cyclone of strength and resolution now.

He grabbed up Dave bodily, ran towards the hut, dropped Dave, closed the door, barred it, and stood panting and trembling with excitement as he proceeded to release his companion.

It was then that Dave Fearless made that fervid remark:

"Mr. Daley, you are a brave man!"

CHAPTER XXVII

THE POISONED DARTS

It was after a brief, hurried conversation that Dave and Daley began an inspection of their surroundings.

"You ask what next?" said Dave, stirring about to ease his cramped limbs and snapping a match. "I think we had first better learn the condition of the enemy."

"Hey, don't do that, lad!" called out Daley quickly, as Dave moved as if to open the barred door and peer out.

"There's no other way of finding out what we want to know," said Dave.

"Yes, there is!" declared Daley. "I just saw a ladder in a corner here. It leads to the roof, I think."

"Try it and see," suggested Dave, which they did.

"All right," announced Daley, as they came out on a square roof like a platform, "we can get a famous idea of the rights of things from here."

Dave surveyed the prospect in great curiosity. The roof resembled an arsenal. There were hundreds and hundreds of all kinds of spears, pikes, and darts.

Some were made up in bundles, some were leaning against the rising parapet as if slanted to catch the sunlight. In the center of the roof was a little raised platform. This held a lot of spears and darts, the heads resting in a big flat bowl full of some dark-colored liquid.

"There they are," announced Dave, glancing down at the spot where they had last seen his recent captors.

Daley, too, viewed the quartette. Two of them had fully recovered from their injuries. One was squatted on the ground, holding his head between his knees and rocking to and fro and moaning.

The fourth lay flat on the ground, still insensible, but the two able natives were rubbing him to restore him to consciousness.

"We're safe enough here," remarked Daley, with some satisfaction. "They can't possibly get in--they won't try."

"No, we seem to have a whole armory at our disposal," said Dave. "Stoodles taught me to use the dart pretty well."

"We could hold those fellows at bay for a long time."

"Just so," nodded Dave, "provided we are not starved out. You know it is folly to think of staying here if we can possibly get away. They would soon bring an army to surround us, and then all chances of escape would be gone."

"I knocked them out once," said Daley. "We'll try it again if you say so. It would be equal chances if those two cowards, Jones and Lewis, hadn't shown the white feather, after promising to join me and help me. The minute I pointed out the natives here to them, they cut stick for dear life."

"Well, they must take care of themselves, after this. Wait, we won't venture out yet, Mr. Daley. See, the fellows have got in trim to challenge us."

The four natives were now fully recovered from Daley's vigorous onslaught, it seemed.

They consulted and chattered, with frequent glances up at the enemy in possession of their stronghold.

One of them, evidently the leader of the group, worked himself up into a perfect fever of excitement and rage.

He approached nearer to the hut and shouted up a loud rigmarole to Dave and Daley. Suddenly wheeling around, he seized a dart from the heap on the litter.

So rapid and expert was he that even though the man dodged, it pierced Daley's cap through and through, showing its tremendous force by carrying the headgear fully twenty feet beyond the roof of the hut.

"Aha, two can play at that game, my friend," said Daley.

He seized a dart and hurled it back at the men. They laughed at him derisively as it struck the ground lightly and harmlessly beyond them. Even Dave had to smile at the sailor's sheer clumsiness.

Now the refugees had to duck down frequently, for all four of the natives began to shower the darts at them.

"I will try a hand," suggested Dave at last. "These on this little platform seem better made than the others. Hi-aa-ooa!" yelled Dave, standing up and poising the dart. He used the great war-cry of the tribe that Pat Stoodles had taught him in a moment of leisure.

The minute Dave raised the weapon a frightful uproar arose from the four men. Their eyes seemed fixed in horror on the poised dart. Like lightning they turned. In a flash they took to the nearest covert and hid themselves.

"Well, well!" cried the amused Daley, "that's a sudden change of front. Lad, there's some meaning to that move."

"Why, yes," said Dave thoughtfully; "they acted as if they were scared to death. I wonder why?"

He paused and turned the dart over in his hand, studying it critically.

"Say, Mr. Daley," he observed, "do you suppose this is some peculiar kind of a weapon that they attach taboo or some of their queer outlandish superstitions to?"

"Drop it!" all of a sudden almost screamed Daley.

He dashed the dart from the hands of his companion in a most startling way.

"Why, Mr. Daley----" began Dave in astonishment.

"Don't you ever go to feeling the points of those darts again, boy," said Daley seriously. "Look here."

He drew Dave nearer to the little platform in the center of the roof.

"I've guessed it out," said Daley. "Yes, it must be so. See that liquid stuff the dart heads are resting in--see the rattlesnake heads in a heap yonder?"

"Why," exclaimed Dave comprehendingly; "poison!"

"Poison of the most deadly kind, lad!" declared Daley. "We've got them now. They won't dare to show their heads as long as we shake one of those poisoned darts at them. Only be careful how you handle them. They are sure, sudden death. One of the Raven crew was struck with one of them in an attack the first time we landed here. He died in an hour."

The camp-fire burned down gradually. Their enemies remained under cover. The clouds grew heavier, and there was finally no moonlight or other illumination of the scene.

"It will be daylight soon," remarked Dave, after a long spell of silence. "Mr. Daley, we mustn't stay here."

"Right, mate. I've been thinking of that myself."

"See here," said Dave, going to the remotest corner of the roof away from the front of the hut. "There's a tree with some branches in reach. Let us take that route. The trees are thick, clear over to what looks like some kind of a corral yonder."

"An excellent idea," voted Daley. "Well, try it, lad."

Dave's suggestion was a pronounced success. They got to the first tree, to a second, to a third. Apparently their escape was unobserved by the natives.

"We're safe enough now," said Daley. "I say, lad, look down. Whatever are those queer-looking animals?"

"Horses," said Dave, straining his gaze at a kind of corral, inside of which half a dozen animals were tethered.

"They don't look United States like," observed Daley.

"No; they are called dadons. They are very rare here, Stoodles told me. I never saw but one before."

"Suppose----" began Daley, descending to the ground. Then suddenly he exclaimed: "They're after us!"

From the nearest bushes some darts cut the air as the two refugees reached the ground. The next moment, showing that they had been aware of their movements all along and were awaiting just this opportunity to attack them, the four weapon-makers burst into view.

"Run for it!" shouted Daley.

"This way," directed Dave, dashing towards the corral. "Out with your knife, Mr. Daley. Cut the tether of one of those dadons. I'll do the same. We may escape those natives yet."

CHAPTER XXVIII

A WILD RIDE

"All aboard, mate!" shouted Daley.

"Keep together," called out Dave.

"It's going to be a tussle," panted the sailor. "My, but she's a skittish one."

Daley had mounted one of the dadons after cutting its tether. Dave had succeeded in landing himself on the back of another.

The dadons were horses in all things except a peculiarly long mane and a head shaped like that of a zebra.

The minute Dave got mounted he managed to form the tether into a kind of a nose loop, but he could get no control of the animal under him. He could simply hold on.

Both dadons were wildly averse to being ridden. That on which Daley rode made a blind dash through the corral ropes, and Dave's animal followed him.

Some darts rained about the fugitives for a minute or two.

Then disappointed howls alone told of the natives they had eluded.

"Try to stop," shouted Dave to Daley, who was in the lead, after they had made a reckless rush of fully two miles across a great level stretch of heather.

But Daley did not hear Dave or was unable to heed him. He kept straight on. The heather ended. A great range of hills presented. As Daley and his steed turned into these, Dave lost sight of them.

He had given a thought to Jones and Lewis and felt it his and Daley's duty to look up the fellows, even if their courage had failed them at a critical moment.

Dave, however, could not stop the dadon he rode. The animal was perfectly uncontrollable. It went like a flash, snorting frightfully, blindly grazing tree branches that hung over the rough route, and once or twice Dave was nearly swept from its back.

He could now only assume that Daley was somewhere ahead, that sooner or later the animal the sailor rode, superior to Dave's own in speed, would tire out and slow down.

"We mustn't become separated," Dave told himself. "Ah, there he is."

Dave caught a flashing view of steed and rider at a break in the hills. Then they disappeared. He held on tightly, hoping his tarpan would follow its mate.

It was now daylight. The scenery about was indescribably wild and grand. Now they had reached a broad and level plateau. There would be a clear space, then a dense timber stretch.

This alternation kept up for many a mile.

"Where is Daley?" was the anxious theme of Dave's thoughts. "I am going to control this animal," he decided doughtily, a minute later.

Dave tried to form the loose end of the tether into some kind of a bridle. Jolted about, forced to cling closely at least with one hand all of the time, however, for fear he would be thrown off, Dave had to abandon this experiment.

"The sea!" he cried suddenly, catching a distant view of it. "That's all right," said Dave. "Whether ahead or behind, Daley will make for the seashore. Maybe he's there now. Whoa! Whoa! I've got to jump. Too late!"

The animal had been dashing down an incline for some time. Emerging from a belt of verdure with startling suddenness, a sheer dip to the edge of a cliff was visible.

The dadon could not stay its course. It fairly slipped the length of the dip. So fast did the animal go that Dave had not time to leave its back before its flying hoofs had struck nothingness.

Forty feet down a dead-water bay showed, dotted with islands. The sensation of descent was one of breathlessness.

The animal struck the water squarely with its forefeet. Steed and rider were borne under completely.

Dave arose, free from the animal at last.

He floated, catching his breath, and saw the dadon swim towards the shore and go scampering out of sight along the wooded beach.

"Well," commented Dave, "here's an adventure. I'm thankful for whole bones. I hope that Daley has fared quite as luckily."

Dave swam ashore. He sat down by some bushes and took off his coat, to dry it in the sun. Under the bushes was plenty of dead wood, and he reached out and secured two pieces to form a sort of clothes-bar.

These he had arranged in due order. Dave reached for a third piece. He seized what he supposed to be a fragment of old wood. It felt soft, yielding, and drew away from his hand with startling suddenness.

"Eh, why," cried Dave. "A human foot!"

The object had disappeared, but there was a rustling under the dense foliage of the bushes.

"I'll have this out," declared Dave, and jumped to his feet and pulled aside the bushes.

Cowering on the ground, his face showing alarm and suffering, a pitiful, pleading look in his eyes, was a dusky native.

"The outcast--the man I saw with the priest of the tribe two days ago," exclaimed Dave. "Yes, it's the same man."

Dave was tremendously worked up at this recognition. He stood regarding the native speculatively. He fully realized that this meeting might mean a great deal to himself and his friends.

Had he not seen the person now before him give a lot of the treasure gold pieces to the priest of the tribe?

Was he not then as now persuaded that the outcast knew where the rest of the treasure was secreted?

"Why," said Dave, "this man holds the key to the whole situation. Now then, my friend, you and I must understand one another."

CHAPTER XXIX

FOUND!

Dave Fearless pulled farther away the bushes that still half-screened the native. The man sat up, and spoke some words feebly. Dave shook his head. The man sank back dejectedly, knowing now that Dave could not understand him.

Dave saw that the man was hurt and helpless. He tried to find out how. The outcast's face expressed some relief as Dave gently lifted one arm and then the other. Then the outcast pointed to one lower limb.

Dave moved this. The man winced. Dave's face grew serious.

"His left leg is broken," said Dave. "Too bad!"

Dave found that the man's kneebone was completely shattered. He seemed to have had a terrible fall. As Dave proceeded with his ministrations gently, the man pointed to the cliff.

"Fell over there, eh?" translated Dave, nodding as the man went on with expressive gestures. "Pursued by many, many. Yes, I see. You want to go farther? That way? The island out there? My man, I don't think you will stand much moving."

Dave spent an hour bathing the injured limb and setting it in splints. It was a crude surgical operation and must have pained the sufferer intensely, but the very fact of kindly attention and treatment seemed to cheer up the poor fellow.

"I've certainly got a new and great responsibility on my hands," thought Dave. "What am I going to do now? If he is recaptured, he will probably be sacrificed. If he is left here alone, he will starve and die of neglect. Yes," said Dave firmly, "black or white, friend or foe, the poor fellow relies on my sympathy. He is going to get it, too, to the fullest extent. I won't desert him."

Dave busied himself looking for food. He hoped that Daley or the other two men might show up. He was near the sea. The Swallow might happen by.

"Well, you're a persistent sort of a fellow," commented Dave, as the outcast for the twentieth time or more pointed to the island he had first indicated in the same pleading way. "What do you want to go there for?"

The outcast put his finger in the sand and traced a boat there.

"Ah, some kind of a craft on that island," guessed Dave. "Do you mean that? All right, I'll investigate."

Dave disrobed and swam to the island the man had pointed out.

He went all over it, and finally, among a thick clump of reeds, he came across a canoe. "Good!" cried Dave, feeling that he had been well rewarded for his care to the sufferer. "Why, it's a splendid little craft, paddles and all. The man must have brought it here and hidden it. He made for this spot when pursued."

When Dave got back to his patient with the canoe, the latter could not conceal his satisfaction and delight.

He motioned Dave to drag the canoe close up to him, which Dave did. He reached over into the bow and pulled out a bag made of skin.

This he handed to Dave with a free, hearty gesture, indicating that it was a gift.

Dave opened the bag. His pulses beat pretty high. His hopes grew immensely.

"More of the gold--the same gold, part of the treasure!" he exclaimed, with glowing eyes. "I was surely right. This man knows all about the treasure."

Dave looked at the outcast speculatively. He wondered how he could make him indicate more. He, too, began tracing in the sand. It was an intricate and laborious task. At the end of an hour Dave looked triumphant.

"It's plain as day!" he cried, preparing the canoe for a voyage. "The man indicates that this gold is a mere sample of what he can produce. It is hidden on an island west. He pokes dots in the outline he draws, as if it is full of caves. He is angry at the treachery of the Windjammers. He will have nothing further to do with them. If I will cure him up, he will take me to the treasure. If I will stay his friend and carry him away from his enemies, he will give up all the gold--all of it. Oh! a famous bargain. Well, I simply must find the Swallow now."

Dave got afloat. He put some soft grasses in the bottom of the canoe and made the invalid comfortable.

They got out to sea, and the youth progressed with some skill, for it was not his first experience with the paddles.

During the ensuing ten hours Dave did not see any craft afloat or person ashore. He kept going north.

"Somewhere along the coast I am bound to run across the Swallow," he confidently told himself.

Dave was utterly worn out as dusk began to come down over land and sea. He did not cease his paddling, however, tired as he was. Some distance away he had made out a familiar landmark.

The shades of night were falling as Dave drove the canoe past the natural curtain of vines that hid the cave for which he was making.

"Oh, see!"

He dropped the paddles and sat like one transfixed. A glorious picture was outlined by a cheerful camp-fire ashore.

It showed animated figures preparing an evening meal--comfort, good cheer, homelikeness.

But most of all, the radiant flare showed the stanch dear old steamer, the Swallow, in a safe harbor and in friendly hands.

CHAPTER XXX

DISASTER

It would be impossible to do full justice to the joy and excitement occasioned by the return of Dave Fearless to the Swallow.

Dave had come up to the steamer unperceived. He knew how to get to the old familiar deck without being discovered.

His first rush was for the dear old father, seated on a stool watching the cheerful scene ashore, but all the time thinking of his missing son.

There was an affectionate greeting between these two who thought so much of one another. Then Captain Broadbeam nearly wrung Dave's hand lame, trying to express his delight at seeing him once more safe and sound aboard the Swallow.

"Mr. Stoodles away--and Bob, too?" exclaimed Dave disappointedly, a little later, as he was told of the happenings with his friends since he had last seen them. "That is unfortunate. I hope they will soon return safely. In fact, it is almost indispensable that Mr. Stoodles see the poor native I brought aboard with me."

"He'll have to see him soon, then," said Doctor Barrell, shaking his head seriously. "The man is in pretty bad condition, Dave. I doubt if I can pull him through."

"He is the possessor of a great secret," said Dave. "Let me tell you about it."

"I hope Stoodles comes back in time to talk with the outcast," said Amos Fearless anxiously, after Dave had told his story.

The next morning there was some disturbing news to report by the boatswain. Gerstein had escaped during the night, taking the best equipped of the small yawls with him.

Then there were two days of solicitous nursing of the outcast and anxious waiting for the return of Stoodles and Bob.

One morning a loud cheer brought the coterie at the captain's table in great haste and excitement on deck.

Stoodles and Bob had arrived by the overland route.

There was a vast babel of talk and welcome lasting over an hour, while all matters were mutually explained.

"I'm so solid with the present government of the Windjammers," boasted Pat proudly, "that I could command legions and phalanxes at my instant beck and call."

"That is good, Mr. Stoodles," smiled Dave. "So you had them out looking everywhere for me, did you?"

"Yes, and I promised them that a fearful visitation of fire--some of Bob's foine fireworks--would disrupt the nation if within three days you were not found."

"Well, Stoodles," said Captain Broadbeam, "we may need the help of the natives when we get farther along. For the present, however, there is only one thing to do. Get into shape to go for that treasure. The Swallow is all fixed up. We are in perfect sailing trim. We know that Nesik and his crowd are still alive, but we need have no fear of them without a ship to harbor them. Another thing--Gerstein's escape is unfortunate. He may get to his friends and warn them. In the morning we will start to hunt up the treasure."

"Gerstein may get there first," suggested Dave.

"Suppose he does. He's got no ship to carry the treasure away in. I see possible fighting ahead if we run across Nesik and the Hankers, but we've got the upper hand of them. Dave, lad, take Stoodles down to see the native you brought here. Try to find out something definite about the hiding-place of the treasure, will you, Pat?"

"Shure, I will," declared Stoodles.

"Oh, the man will tell you freely--I know it from his gestures to me!" declared Dave. "He was very low last night, though. Come, Mr. Stoodles, I will take you to him, let him know that you are my friend, and the rest will be easy."

They went to the forecastle. The boatswain met them at the door of the little compartment that marked the hospital of the ship.

"Mr. Stoodles is to see the sick native, Mr. Drake," said Dave.

The boatswain looked very somber.

"Mr. Stoodles is too late," he pronounced solemnly.

"Too late?" echoed Dave.

"Yes; the poor fellow died an hour ago."

Dave went back to the cabin with the sad news. Stoodles expressed a curiosity to see the outcast, and the boatswain accompanied him to the hospital.

When later Dave looked for Pat, the Milesian sent word by the boatswain that he was very busy and would see his friend in the morning.

It was about two hours after midnight that Dave awoke with a great start. As he sprang to the floor from his berth Bob Vilett dashed into the stateroom.

"Dave, Dave!" he cried. "It's all up with us."

"Now what----" began Dave. He was interrupted by great tramping on the deck and the sound of pistol-shots.

Dave hurried on his clothes and rushed after Bob to the deck.

A blow from a marlinspike sent Bob flat and a rough stranger grabbed Dave as he appeared.

Captain Broadbeam and his crew were hemmed in near the bow, held at bay by a dozen armed men.

With a sinking heart Dave realized what had happened--the brave little Swallow was in the hands of their enemies: Captain Nesik of the Raven, the Hankers, and all that rascally crew.

CHAPTER XXXI

A LUCKY FIND

"Land ahead!" sang out Captain Broadbeam's terrific voice in foghorn bass.

"We'll never reach it," declared Bob Vilett.

"Begorra, this is the worst yet," observed Pat Stoodles.

"Steady; be ready to jump if the raft tips," said Dave Fearless.

Fog, blackness, rain, and tempest surrounded the crew of the Swallow. A critical moment, indeed, had arrived in their experiences.

The capture of the Swallow early that morning had been effected by their enemies within an hour. The attack had been a vast surprise. No one had anticipated it, no one was prepared to meet it.

Superior numbers, desperate men heavily armed, had simply overpowered those on board of the steamer two at a time.

The bound captives were put ashore. With sad hearts they saw the Swallow sail out of the secret cove in the hands of their enemies. Dave's hardest trial was to listen to the triumphant taunts of Bart Hankers. The elder Hankers gloated over Amos Fearless.

Captain Nesik goaded Captain Broadbeam to the verge of madness with his mean sneers.

Then they steamed away, the captives got loose from their bonds, and there they were, faced with the very worst fortune, it seemed, where a few hours previous good luck only had smiled on them.

"I've an idea," said Pat Stoodles at once.

"Well, what is it?" asked Broadbeam.

"Put afther the rascals."

"Of course we will do that," said the captain, "and mighty smart, too. Don't give up, lads," he cried encouragingly to those around him. "We've the will, we'll find a way. Something tells me those thieving buccaneers haven't the intelligence or grit to hold a good point when they make it."

"Captain," said Stoodles, with a sudden air of importance, "if you will all come to the native village with me, I'll bargain to have you conveyed where you like in all the royal canoes of the tribe."

"It would take too much time--it might complicate matters. The sight of so many of us might change the ideas of the natives as to a friendly welcome," said Broadbeam.

"Why not make a raft, then?" suggested Doctor Barrell.

"Where to go?" asked Bob Vilett, who was quite dejected over the bad turn in affairs.

"In search of the threasure, shure," said Pat.

"We don't know where it is," said Bob. "We might search for forty years and not find a trace of the treasure."

"Not at all," put in Dave sharply. "Find an island full of caves, and we have the location. I am sure of that from what the outcast native imparted to me."

"And I," announced Pat Stoodles suddenly. "Begorra, I'm the lad who can put my finger right on the one particular cave where the threasure is stored."

All hands looked at Stoodles in a sort of dubious amazement.

"Is that true, Mr. Stoodles?" asked Doctor Barrell.

"Shure it is."

"How can you know that?" inquired Dave.

"The outcast tould me."

"Told you. Why, he was dead when you saw him," said Dave.

"The outcast tould me," reiterated Pat solemnly. "Not another wurred now. I am spaking from facts. Get afloat, make for the lasht of the three western islands. Land me. I'll take you to the threasure blindfold."

They set to work at once to make a raft. This was not difficult, for plenty of excellent material was at hand. It was late afternoon when they got afloat. At ten o'clock that evening, caught in a terrible storm, the appearance of breakers denoted the nearness of land.

"Jump for your lives!" suddenly rang out the voice of Captain Broadbeam.

The raft had struck an immense rock and was splintered to pieces by the contact. Now it was a wild swim for shore in the boiling surf.

Captain Broadbeam anxiously and eagerly counted his men a few minutes later as they ranged on the beach.

"None lost," he announced gladly. "Where are we, Stoodles?"

"I can't exactly tell, your honor, but I should say on the second western island. I'll take a short trip and report, sir."

Stoodles strolled away in one direction; Dave, ever active, went in another.

In half an hour Stoodles was back to the little group of refugees with the statement that they were on the second west island, as he had guessed before.

"Dave seems to be gone a long time," observed Amos Fearless, after an hour had passed by, during which they all busied themselves in securing such pieces of the wrecked raft as came ashore.

Suddenly Dave appeared. He was out of breath, he had been running fast. Something of suppressed excitement in his manner showed itself plainly.

"What are you saving all that wreckage for?" he asked Bob Vilett.

"Why, to make a new raft, of course."

"Don't waste your time," advised Dave, with a quick, glad laugh. "Captain, father, men, follow me! I've found the Swallow."

"What!" shouted Captain Broadbeam, transfixed.

"She is anchored not a mile to the north. Six men left in charge of her are all stupid with drink on her deck. I crept aboard, bound them all, and the Swallow is ours once more."

CHAPTER XXXII

CONCLUSION

"What are the sticks for, Mr. Stoodles?" asked Dave Fearless.

"Shure, they're reed torches."

"Oh, we have to have a light, have we?" asked Bob Vilett.

"Shure, ye have. It's simmering darkness we're going into."

"This is the famous cave island, is it?" said Dave. "Well, it deserves the name. Why, it's a regular honeycomb."

"No sign of Nesik and the others yet," said Captain Broadbeam. "I wonder what has become of them?"

"That's aisy to surmise, captain," declared Pat Stoodles. "They left the fellows aboard the Swallow to guzzle and get sthupid while they took a yawl and came here to remove the threasure."

"Yes, you must remember," said Dave, "that their whole plan all along has been to delude their crew into the belief that the treasure went down in the Swallow.'"

"Wan, two, three, four, five," spoke Stoodles, patrolling a patch of beach, and looking up and counting along the immense row of fissures and openings in the solid rock. "The lasht one I indicate is the place we must go into."

"You mean to say," observed Dave, "that the treasure is hidden in that cave."

"Thanks to you I mane to say it, and sthick to it, too, my brave lad," cried Pat exuberantly.

"Thanks to me?" repeated Dave blankly.

"Begorra, yes."

"You puzzle me, Mr. Stoodles."

"Arrah, then, out with it: The outcast was dead when I saw him, but I happened to notice that his back was tattooed. It took me eight hours to make out the marks. I can spake the native dialect well enough, but the script was hard to figure out. But I did it."

"And what did it tell?" asked Dave interestedly.

"Well, two outcasts had found the gold. So as not to forget exactly where it was, one tattooed a diagram or chart, or whatever you may call it, on the back of the other. One of them died a little later. That's all, come on."

The wonders of the next two hours, those who followed the guidance of Pat Stoodles never forgot. It was like a visit to fairy-land. They penetrated underground chambers of dazzling magnificence, the torches illuminating walls and roofs of glittering splendor.

At last, in a depression of a great rock-crystal stone, they came across a heap of straw.

Pulling it aside, a golden gleam dazzled the eager eyes of the onlookers.

"It's there! Oh, it's there!" cried the enraptured Dave Fearless.

The ocean treasure, again recovered, lay before them.

It had come so easily, so naturally, that there was something unreal about the whole thing.

The moment could not help but be filled with the intensest joy and excitement. Yet in a plain, practical, business way they went to work to encase the great mountain of loose golden coins in sacks which they had brought with them.

It was nightfall when they had got the golden hoard all on board of the Swallow, and safely stored in the hold of the stanch little steamer that had carried them through so many adventures and perils in safety up to this supreme moment of their lives.

What of Nesik and his cohorts? Fifty times during the evening this theme was earnestly discussed.

Dave Fearless sat thinking over this and many other things late that night, enjoying the cool, refreshing breeze as he lay comfortably in a hammock.

Suddenly he jumped upright with a shock. A form dripping with water clambered into view. He landed on the deck, staring wildly about him.

"Someone, quick!" he gasped. "I'm done out. Quick, Fearless! Start the steamer, quick! Danger--explosion!"

"Daley!" shouted Dave. And then, as the man fell like a clod at his feet, he ran right down into the engine room.

Something told Dave that this man was giving an important friendly warning.

He fairly pulled Bob Adams from his bunk. He ordered him to start the engines at once. He ran to the cabin and roused Captain Broadbeam.

"What's this--the steamer going?" cried Broadbeam.

"Yes, something is wrong," gasped Dave. "Come on deck--the mischief!"

A frightful roar rent the air. The whole ship shivered. Just behind him as he came up on deck Dave saw a mighty flare, a great lifting of the waters. Then all was still.

It was not until the following morning, when Daley recovered consciousness, that they knew the terrible peril they had escaped through his friendly intervention.

It seemed that he had managed to get to the second west island. He was nearly starved when he ran across Nesik and the others.

He decided it was politic to make friends with them. The night previous he was the only trusted one of the crew that Nesik and the Hankers took in the yawl that went for the treasure.

"They got the gold," narrated Daley.

"Oh, they did?" muttered Captain Broadbeam, with a jolly smile.

"I helped them--in bags just as Gerstein had left it."

"Smart boy, that same Gerstein!" chuckled Pat Stoodles.

"Then they discovered that you people had recaptured the Swallow," continued Daley. "All day they hid with the yawl in a little cave. They decided you people would be too watchful to ever afford them a chance to again get possession of the steamer. You certainly would try to find them. Gerstein submitted a diabolical plan. They had some dynamite used in clearing away a stopped-up passageway in the cave. They made up a float, fused the dynamite, and with a cord guided it down the beach towards you. I got away from them."

"And warned us in time, brave mate!" cried Captain Broadbeam, heartily grasping the sailor's hand. "We're your friends for life."

The Swallow did not leave the Windjammers' Island for a week. During that time Stoodles made several visits to the natives. On one of these he and Dave took with them the two boxes Dave had purchased at Minotaur Island.

They returned feeling pretty good over something accomplished, and refused to discuss it with the intensely curious Bob Vilett.

Jones and Lewis were found and taken aboard of the Swallow, which started homeward-bound at last.

At Mercury Island their prisoners from the Raven were set ashore. Of Captain Nesik, the Hankers, and the others not a trace had been found.

Dave and his friends well knew that a terrible disappointment had faced the plotters when they came to discover that the bags they had secured in one of the caves did not contain the gold.

The native outcasts they were certain had removed the gold to the place where they found it, filling the bags with something heavy and replacing these at the original hiding-place.

Amos Fearless gave his friends a royal banquet the day the Swallow arrived at San Francisco.

Each one, down to the humblest sailor, received a generous share of the ocean treasure they had suffered so much to secure.

The rest of the gold was shipped by rail to Quanatack, and Doctor Barren's curiosities to the Government at Washington.

Captain Broadbeam, Doctor Barrell, Pat Stoodles, and Bob Vilett were special guests of Dave and his father in the new beautiful home they bought on Long Island Sound.

"Dave, when are you ever going to tell us that secret of yours and Stoodles' about those two boxes you took from Minotaur Island?" asked Bob one evening, as they all sat on the broad veranda of the Fearless home, enjoying the lovely evening.

"Oh, that is only a side issue now," smiled Dave, "seeing we got the treasure."

"A great scheme, though," said Stoodles. "I'll tell it. Dave simply got the royal sanction at the Windjammers' Island to establish a postal service. We did it up officially before the whole tribe. We printed ten thousand postage stamps."

"And as we control the whole issue," said Dave, "of course we can charge our own price for them as rarities."

The old ocean diver and his son were sorry when their loyal friends had to leave them for the duties of life that called them to business.

They saw much of one another, however, from time to time. Each was splendidly provided for out of the ocean treasure. Good fortune did not spoil any of them, and each settled down to a practical, useful, and happy life.

THE END

9 781836 573616